"You're a stranger in the hollow. For safety reasons, you shouldn't wander without an escort."

One eyebrow rose, challenging Jo's explanation. The reporter shoved away from the post and descended another step, and another, until his naked chest was inches from her face. "You're afraid I'll run into Lightning Jack, is that it?"

"No." She licked her suddenly dry lips. Sullivan was nice, sexy and dangerous—a lethal combination. He unnerved her, unbalanced her, frustrated her, yet excited her, too. Being close to him for any length of time would cause tremendous grief, stress—and bouts of arousal.

She was afraid for herself.

Dear Reader,

I hope you enjoy journeying into the Appalachian Mountains for my next Harlequin American Romance series, HEARTS OF APPALACHIA. The Appalachians are America's oldest mountain range and extend from Maine to Georgia. The mountains, whose forests date back 300 million years, are comprised of razorbacked ridges that plunge into deep, beautiful "hollers."

This series focuses on a Scotch-Irish clan whose ancestors first settled eastern Kentucky in the 1730s. Due to the insular nature of these beautiful mountains, people have retained many ancestral traditions, which they showcase through their unique language, art, religion, spirit and attitude. Many people of Appalachia are independent and resistant to change, are committed to taking care of their own and harbor a deep mistrust of strangers—as does the heroine in this book, Jo Macpherson. Her goal to educate the younger generation about the value of their ancestry is challenged by none other than a flatlander—Sullivan Mooreland, a Seattle newspaper reporter intent on sensationalizing Jo's clan by running a story on their infamous bootlegger Lightning Jack.

Sit back and watch the sparks fly as these two determined people from vastly different worlds go head-to-head and find love off the beaten path.

Please visit me at www.marinthomas.com for information on the next two titles in my HEARTS OF APPALACHIA series: *In a Soldier's Arms*, available January 2008, and *A Coal Miner's Wife*, available July 2008.

Happy reading!

Marin

For the Children
MARIN THOMAS

TORONTO • NEW YORK • LONDON
AMSTERDAM • PARIS • SYDNEY • HAMBURG
STOCKHOLM • ATHENS • TOKYO • MILAN • MADRID
PRAGUE • WARSAW • BUDAPEST • AUCKLAND

ISBN-13: 978-0-373-75188-4
ISBN-10:   0-373-75188-5

FOR THE CHILDREN

This edition published by arrangement with Harlequin Books S.A.

® and TM are trademarks of the publisher. Trademarks indicated with
® are registered in the United States Patent and Trademark Office, the
Canadian Trade Marks Office and in other countries.

www.eHarlequin.com

Printed in U.S.A.

ABOUT THE AUTHOR

Typical of small-town kids, all Marin Thomas, born in Janesville, Wisconsin, could think about was how to leave after she graduated from high school.

Her six-foot-one-inch height was her ticket out. She accepted a basketball scholarship at the University of Missouri in Columbia, where she studied journalism. After two years she transferred to U of A at Tucson, where she played center for the Lady Wildcats. While at Arizona, she developed an interest in fiction writing and obtained a B.A. in radio-television. Marin was inducted in May 2005 into the Janesville Sports Hall of Fame for her basketball accomplishments.

Her husband's career in public relations has taken them to Arizona, California, New Jersey, Colorado, Texas and Illinois, where she currently calls Chicago her home. Marin can now boast that she's seen what's "out there." Amazingly enough, she's a living testament to the old adage "You can take the girl out of the small town, but you can't take the small town out of the girl." Her heart still lies in small-town life, which she loves to write about in her books.

Books by Marin Thomas

HARLEQUIN AMERICAN ROMANCE

1024—THE COWBOY AND THE BRIDE
1050—DADDY BY CHOICE
1079—HOMEWARD BOUND
1124—AARON UNDER CONSTRUCTION*
1148—NELSON IN COMMAND*
1175—RYAN'S RENOVATION*

*The McKade Brothers

This book is for the Bailey women:
Barbara, Jill, Jennifer and Jeanna.

Each unique in your own way.
Barbara, the family cheerleader.
Jill, the compassionate caregiver.
Jennifer, the explorer and entrepreneur.
Jeanna, the warrior queen, whose strength
and courage never cease to amaze me.

Grandma Smith would be so proud.

Chapter One

The last thing Johanna Macpherson expected to encounter on the winding Kentucky mountain road was a gussied-up flatlander.

Leaning forward, she pressed her bosom to the steering wheel and slowed the pickup for a better look-see at the stranger running like a skinned cat from her neighbor's pack of coonhounds. Suit tails flapping in the wind and tie ringing his neck, the "cat" was losing ground fast. *Served the man right if the pack treed him.*

She'd been taught from a young age not to trust flatlanders—anyone not born on the mountain. She'd never understood the clan's suspicion of strangers—until she'd attended the University of Kentucky in Lexington and discovered that people weren't always what they appeared to be.

Some lessons had to be learned the hard way.

As she pulled the pickup even with the stranger, she noticed his face was redder than a prize-winning tomato and his cheeks puffed like a steam locomotive. The poor idiot was plumb tuckered. After retrieving the shotgun from under the bench seat, she pointed the barrel out the passenger window, then blasted the truck horn.

The stranger glanced at her. His eyes widened until only the whites were visible and then he dived into the mess of baby cattails growing in the ditch. *Good grief.* Did he expect her to shoot *him?* Jo aimed the gun skyward and fired. The hounds scattered—except Beauregard. She steered the truck to the side of the road.

Weapon in hand, she traipsed back to where the stranger had taken cover. If it was possible to lick a human to death, then Beauregard had accomplished the feat. All one hundred pounds of beagle-foxhound mix rested on the man's chest, while his long, pink tongue laved the stranger from neck to hairline. The flatlander played possum—attempted to, anyway—but the fool forgot to hold his breath.

Amused, Jo propped the shotgun on her hip and tugged the brim of her floppy felt hat lower to shield her eyes from the midafternoon sun. The man's face was lean and angular, in contrast to his large mouth. Thick brows, several shades darker than his tussled wheat-colored hair, slashed across his forehead. Not a handsome face, but an interesting one, nonetheless. Jo stuck her fingers in her mouth and whistled. Beau's ears perked and he sprang from his perch, eliciting a loud *oomph!* from the possum.

"Go!" She pointed to the woods, and Beau bounded up the hill. Leveling the rifle at the trespasser's heart, she asked, "How long you planning to lie there like a carcass?"

One eye—brown in color—cracked open. "Depends."

"On what?"

"On whether there's any shot left in that gun."

"I got shot left, mister."

"You going to use it on me?"

"Depends."

"On…"

"What business you have in our hollow."

"Your hollow?" Grunting, the interloper rolled to his knees

and hauled himself to his feet. Tall, he towered over Jo's five feet six inches.

Not until he cleared his throat did she realize she'd been caught checking him out. Well, phooey. She hadn't come in contact with a man this… Okay, he was sort of attractive. *Never mind.* "This side of the mountain is private property."

Eyes narrowed on the gun, he inquired, "You any good with that thing?"

Jo aimed at the woods, took a bead on her target, then fired. A pinecone exploded from the branch of a tree.

The flatlander swallowed hard. "My car ran out of gas. I was returning to town—" he motioned behind her "—until the dogs showed up out of nowhere. Then I switched directions." He pointed over his shoulder. "My car's parked around the bend."

"I've got a gas can in the truck. Meet you there."

Without affording him an opportunity to respond, she hopped into the pickup and sped off. She glanced in the rear-view mirror and grinned at the trespasser's whopper-jawed gape.

Did he expect her to give a stranger a lift? As soon as she rounded the curve in the road, she spotted the car. A red Corvette. Typical hoity-toity flatlander vehicle—useless. She parked behind the sports car, hopped out of the truck and grabbed the gas can. Ten seconds later she swore under her breath. The blasted gas-tank door was locked. So much for her plan to be gone by the time the owner caught up.

She considered leaving the fuel and driving off, but there was something wily about the stranger that kept her feet planted. At least, that was what she told herself rather than admit she wouldn't mind another gander at the man who'd made her heart go *thumpity-bump.*

A few minutes passed and he came into view, his face scrunched. Squashing her lips together to keep from smiling at his annoyed expression, she stuck her arm through the truck window and placed her hand on the shotgun—a person couldn't be too careful these days.

"Thanks for the lift," he spat, then removed his keys from his pants pocket, directed the fob at the car and bleeped open the gas door. Ignoring her, he set to filling the tank.

"What brings you up here?" she asked.

Silence.

Okay, maybe she wasn't Ms. Ambassador for the Appalachian Mountains Tourist Bureau, but she'd loaned him her gas can. "If you'd state your business, I might be of help."

His chest expanded with a deep breath, which he held for more than the count of three, before he released the air in a noisy burst. With purposeful movements, he capped the can, shut the tank door and faced her, his mouth twisting in a cynical grimace. Just like a city slicker, showing emotion in front of a stranger. "Heather's Hollow."

Fortunately for Jo she had practice concealing her emotions from people she didn't trust. After that slip, the stranger was definitely in the don't-trust category.

"I stopped at the post office in Finnegan's Stand. The clerk wasn't much help. Nodded to the mountain and mumbled, 'Up there.'" The man stowed the empty gas container in the truck bed. "I've been driving in circles for the past hour and a half. You're the first person I've run across on this road."

Not a surprise. Folks tended to remain at home with their families on Sunday afternoons. Seeing how it was a warm end-of-April day, she suspected several of the clan's men had headed for the banks of the Black River to tickle trout.

The stranger stopped before her and Jo swore she caught the scent of cologne—a musky, warm smell that made her want to stand on tiptoe and sniff his neck. He dug his wallet from his pants pocket and held out two twenty-dollar bills. When she didn't accept the cash, he added, "For the gas—" he ran his gaze up and down her tattered overalls "—and whatever else."

First he'd trespassed on her mountain. Second he'd insulted her with an offer of money for lending a helping hand. And third he could have pretended not to notice her ragged work clothes. *Johanna Macpherson, since when have you cared what a man thinks of your appearance?*

"And—" he wiggled the bills under her nose "—for scaring off the dogs."

Accepting a stranger's cash didn't sit right with Jo. But if taking the payment sent the man on his way... She removed one bill from his fingers. "The dog-scaring was complimentary."

He smirked, showing off big white teeth and a hint of a dimple.

Forcing her gaze from the sexy little pit in his right cheek, she asked, "What do you want with Heather's Hollow?"

"Sullivan Mooreland from Seattle." He held out a hand. "I'm a reporter for the *Seattle Courier* newspaper." When Jo ignored his hand, he shoved his fingers through his mussed hair, sending bits of dry grass and weeds floating into the air. "I'm covering a story for the paper."

Six years ago, Jo had been betrayed in the worst way, producing a heightened sense of suspicion when it came to strangers. "What kind of story?"

His eyes flooded with indecision, changing the color to dark chocolate. *Fascinating.* She wondered if Sullivan Mooreland realized the brown orbs broadcast his emotions. He glanced up the road. Then down the road. Then into the ditch alongside the road. Finally determining that they were alone, he whispered, "Lightning Jack. I intend to interview the famous bootlegger."

Stomach churning like flash-flood waters, she asked, "And you believe you'll find him here?"

"My research claims Lightning Jack is a member of the Scotch-Irish clan that lives in Heather's Hollow. I intend to question his relatives and neighbors regarding his activities and whereabouts."

Panic escalated inside her. "Your sources are wrong, mister." She didn't need a big-city reporter sniffing for information on the local legend. Corralling her jumbled nerves, she fibbed, "Last I heard, Lightning Jack lives on the other side of the tunnel."

"What tunnel?"

"Cumberland Gap Tunnel." Jo remembered her grandfather praising the construction of the tunnel that carries U.S. 25E under the Cumberland Gap National Historical Park near the intersection of Kentucky, Tennessee and Virginia. He'd claimed the original trail through the Cumberland Gap belonged to the clans whose ancestors had settled the area, and not to tourists and hippie hikers.

"What's on the other side of the tunnel?" the reporter asked.

"Tennessee."

"None of my research suggested that the bootlegger might be found in Tennessee."

Jo quirked an eyebrow. "Last I heard he moved down there because people kept pestering him."

"Then I'd guess he's living under a false name."

"La—"

"Right," he interrupted. "Last you heard. Once I clear the tunnel, what direction do I head?"

"Thirty-two south until you cross the Clinch River." And to irritate the man further, she added, *"Last I heard* he's hunkered down somewhere along the riverbank."

The flatlander's narrow-eyed stare accused her of being a dog-faced liar, which she was. Still, she took exception. By the time he searched the fourteen-mile stretch of woods hugging the river, he'd be too exhausted to care about finding his *story*.

"All right." He straightened his shoulders. "Since you're the only person who's offered me the time of day, I'll have to accept your word that Lightning Jack isn't here."

What did the stranger expect when he'd driven a hot-rod sports car into a small mountain holler? The clanpeople didn't take kindly to outsiders snooping in their backyard. They were a proud, independent group who watched after their own and out of necessity harbored a deep mistrust of strangers.

"I'm on my way to town. I'll follow you," Jo announced. He hesitated, his frustration burning into her. Did he honestly believe she'd leave him unsupervised? She cranked the truck engine and waited for the road-weary fool to get into his Corvette.

During the drive down the winding mountain road, the reporter checked his rearview mirror several times, and Jo suspected he hoped she'd turn off before they reached Finnegan's Stand. She had to give the guy credit. Unlike her boyfriend in college, who'd treated her with a false sweetness, the outsider didn't hesitate to show displeasure with her. She admired his honesty—and his interesting face. Too bad he was a city slicker. The Corvette stopped at the one-lane wooden bridge extending across Periwinkle Creek.

Was he reconsidering? Maybe a nudge… Her truck crept up to within an inch of his car's bumper before she punched the brake. What had gotten into her? If the pickup so much as nicked the fender of the sports car, he'd contact the state patrol and file a report with his insurance company.

A vehicle approached on the other side of the bridge—Tom Kavenagh, the clan blacksmith. Tom waved the stranger through, leaving the reporter no choice but to continue. When the Corvette exited the other side. Jo put the truck in Reverse and signaled for Tom to cross first.

The blacksmith stopped alongside her. "Trouble, Jo?"

"Nope. Trouble's leaving."

"I'M THIRTY-EIGHT-YEARS OLD. What the hell am I doing schlepping through the Appalachian Mountains, searching for an old-timer who's probably developed some sort of dementia and believes he's Daniel Boone now," Sullivan muttered as the town—rather, map dot—of Finnegan's Stand disappeared in the rearview mirror.

Finnegan's Stand. Crazy name. Sounded like a vegetable lean-to on a rural road. Eight hundred twenty-seven residents and seven businesses—a bank, hardware store, beauty shop, post office, café, grocery mart, gas station and a church with a white steeple rising above the tops of poplar, oak and ash trees. The entire Stand could fit into one city block of downtown Seattle, with room left over for a parking garage.

Stomach churning, Sullivan decided he should have bought a burger at Scooter's Café after he'd filled his tank. His last meal had been earlier in the morning—a burrito from a convenience store in western Kentucky. He suspected nerves and not indigestion were the cause of his gastrointestinal discomfort—and a certain stubborn, know-it-all, smart-mouthed redhead. Never before had Sullivan retreated from following a lead on a story. Why had he allowed the mulish woman to intimidate him? Because she could shoot a pine-cone out of a tree at a hundred yards.

Three days ago, his editor had announced his retirement. Sullivan had assumed he was next in line for the promotion, then discovered the newspaper's editor in chief, Howard Baker, planned to interview an outsider for the position.

Angered that his years of dedication and sacrifice had been

overlooked, Sullivan had resolved to take matters into his own hands. He was certain winning the Monterey Award for best feature story of the year would gain Howard's attention. After hours of rummaging through his *idea* files, Sullivan had stumbled across an old FBI report of Lightning Jack's moonshine activity in the Appalachian Mountains of Kentucky. The article identified the bootlegger as a descendant of the Scotch-Irish clan that had settled near Finnegan's Stand in the early 1700s.

Sullivan had asked Ed, his coworker, to join him in the search for the notorious criminal, but Ed had declined the invitation, choosing family over career. Sullivan didn't understand. What did it matter that the man's wife was pregnant and due any day—with their fourth kid? Sullivan would have expected the whole labor-and-delivery experience to grow old after the first time, but what did he know? He wasn't a father, nor did he intend to be one.

In Sullivan's opinion, family was overrated. He'd grown up with a single mom who'd alternated between binge drinking and minimum-wage jobs that never covered the rents for seedy apartments. Once in a while they'd lived in a car or homeless shelter. His mother had passed away several years ago and he'd been more relieved than sad that he was alone in the world.

He monitored the road signs as he followed the crazy mountain woman's directions to the tunnel. The female bully nagged at him. He hadn't gotten a good glimpse of her face because of the floppy hat that had covered half her head, but she sure filled out those scruffy overalls nicely. He'd considered asking her to remove the boater to see her eyes and determine for himself if she'd told the truth, but he was no match for the loaded shotgun propped against her hip. He thought back to the few women he'd dated in the past. None had ever stood up to him the way the redhead had. If nothing else, she was an enigma—one he wished he had time to investigate.

The entire area consisted of switchbacks, straightaways and hairpin curves. No wonder the Cumberland Gap had been called Massacre Mountain during the late 1700s when the Wilderness Road was used as the main route through the Appalachians. He imagined entire wagon trains plummeting over the edge of steep dropoffs.

Ten miles later he spotted the tunnel, and the tension eased in his gut. Obeying the posted speed limit, he slowed to forty-five miles per hour as he entered the tubular passageway. A sign boasting the Volunteer State greeted him when he zipped out the other end. Another mile and a marker appeared, indicating the turnoff for the Clinch River.

As he drove the fourteen-mile stretch of water, he scanned the dense foliage along the banks, surmising a person might search for months and never find a single living soul in the thick vegetation. Frustrated, he swung in to the first gas station he came across, topped off the tank—he didn't intend to run out of gas again—then entered the Quick Mart.

"Howdy, stranger," a codger greeted him, one cheek bulging with tobacco.

In no mood for niceties, Sullivan approached the counter and grumped, "I'm searching for Lightning Jack. You wouldn't happen to have directions to his place, would you?"

The man's face froze.

"I have it on good authority—" not that Sullivan considered the unknown, shotgun-toting female an authority "—that the bootlegger lives along the banks of the Clinch River."

The wad of tobacco migrated to the other cheek pocket. "Ya gotta name, mister?"

"Sullivan Mooreland."

The clerk's gaze wandered to the red Corvette parked outside. "Ya ain't from these parts."

No kidding. "Seattle, Washington."

The geezer stuck his tongue in the space between his front teeth and worked a piece of tobacco loose. "Yer drivin' in the wrong direction." He wiggled his middle finger westward.

Ha, ha. If Sullivan allowed it, the old fart would dance a jig around him. "I'm doing a feature story on Lightning Jack for the *Seattle Courier* newspaper."

"He know yer comin'?"

"It's a surprise."

"Some folk don't take kindly to surprises."

"Can you tell me what stretch of the river Lightning Jack inhabits?"

"Nope. I ain't ever heard of him livin' this fer down the mountain."

Sullivan's neck itched—a signal he'd been duped. "You wouldn't happen to recall his last place of residence, would you?"

"His clan folk live in Heather's Holler. Ya check there?"

The itching increased in intensity. "Where exactly is the *holler?*"

"Up the mountain from Finnegan's Stand. Soon as ya cross Periwinkle Creek yer in the holler."

Fisting his hands at his sides, Sullivan resisted the urge to punch the Frito bag in the display by the counter. "You're positive?"

Two bushy eyebrows formed a single band of white fuzz across the old coot's brow. "Ya callin' me a liar?"

Before his anger got him busted, Sullivan offered, "Appreciate the information," then left the store. He made a U-turn, sped out of the parking lot and drove back toward the tunnel. After he put a few miles between him and the gas station, he cruised onto the shoulder of the road and cut the engine. With careful, controlled movements, he exited the car, walked several feet away, raised his fist to the sky and shouted, "Shh.....iii...ttt!"

Conned by a backwoods, smart-mouthed hillbilly—or, if he was going to be politically correct, a bluegrass American. He was losing his edge. Served him right for spending less and less time out on the streets, covering a beat. Too many hours behind the desk had softened his instincts. *Damn. Damn. Damn.* Once his anger cooled, he removed his suit jacket and loosened his tie. He'd worn the suit because he'd wanted to appear a respectable and legitimate employee of the media. He hadn't expected that the formal clothes would damage his credibility.

By the time he returned to Finnegan's Stand, the setting sun had left a smear of pink across the horizon. The lit storefronts provided illumination along the main street. Two vehicles were parked in front of Scooter's Café. He'd better eat something, so if he encountered the infamous redheaded tour guide, he wouldn't be tempted to gnaw off her head for sending him on a wild-goose chase.

He parked the 2000 Corvette next to a 1970-something truck with both fenders missing and a cracked windshield. He should have left the sports car at home and flown to Kentucky, then rented a sedan. Living in the city didn't allow for long excursions in the car, so he'd jumped at the chance to drive the 'Vette cross-country.

For a kid who'd grown up wearing church-donated clothing and locker-room sneakers that had gone unclaimed at the end of the school year, the Corvette was Sullivan's nicest possession ever. He'd saved five years for the car. Lived in basement apartments and eaten canned beans and hotdogs in order to make the minimum monthly payment.

When Sullivan entered the café, a giant stuffed bear head greeted him. Sporting a camouflage baseball cap, mouth wide-open and yellow teeth barred, the trophy head decorated the wall above the cash register. The dining area consisted of six tables with red-checkered cloths. A single chandelier made of elk horns hung from the ceiling. His gaze shifted to the lunch counter on the other side of the room, where two couples conversed over coffee and pie.

A waitress—the size of Paul Bunyan—glared at him. No hello. No howdy. Nothing. Sullivan slid onto a stool at the end of the counter.

"I'll take a Dr Pepper," he said, adding a smile to his order.

"Pop machine's busted."

"Coffee smells good." He dared the waitress to ignore him.

Mouth turned down, she grumbled, "Kitchen's closed, but we got apple pie or peach cobbler."

Sullivan was hungry enough to eat raw hamburger. "Apple pie. Thanks—" he read the name tag pinned to the blue smock "—Betty Sue."

Betty Sue placed a cup of blistering-hot coffee on the counter, then disappeared into the kitchen. Sullivan hated coffee. Had since the day his mother had forced him to drink the stuff because she couldn't afford milk. No money for milk, but she'd always found cash to buy coffee to help sober her up before work. He preferred soda. Dr Pepper, mostly—but he'd drink Coke or Pepsi in a pinch.

Since there wasn't much he could salvage from his excursion into Tennessee, he directed his comment to the other patrons. "Nice evening."

The women flashed shy smiles before dropping their gazes to their dessert plates. The men frowned. After the day he'd had, Sullivan felt ornery enough to ruffle a few feathers. "Any of you acquainted with a man named Lighting Jack?"

Silence—until Betty Sue *thunked* the plate of apple pie on the counter. There was no doubt in his mind the waitress knew the bootlegger. Why else would she act hostile? "I heard the man lives in Heather's Hollow." *Silence.* "Drove up the mountain earlier today, but a woman—" he paused for emphasis and was rewarded by the stiffening of Betty Sue's shoulders "—sent me to Tennessee after the bootlegger."

He gobbled the pie, then tossed a five-dollar bill on the counter and stood. "Appreciate the conversation." He paused outside the café, wondering where the hell to go. Finnegan's Stand didn't have a motel. Maybe he'd drive up into the hollow until he found a safe spot at which to park along the road. He and his mother had lived in a car for days at a time. One night in the front seat of the Corvette wouldn't kill him.

With care, he drove slowly and hugged the inside lane of the narrow road until he encountered the bridge. The rickety structure reminded him of days gone past. Way past— horse-and-buggy past. He navigated the planks, praying the weathered boards would hold and he and the car wouldn't plunge into the water a hundred feet below. Once he cleared the bridge, pitch-blackness greeted him. At the base of the mountain, the lights of Finnegan's Stand twinkled in the rear-view mirror. Darkness ahead…light behind. Crazy mountain woman ahead…unfriendly people behind. Not much of a choice. Into the doom and gloom he drove.

Aside from animal-shaped shadows sprinting across the road, Sullivan encountered no other trace of life. Not even a house or a signpost…as if the people living in the hollow disappeared at sundown.

When he passed the spot where he'd run out of gas earlier in the day, he decided to continue, hoping he'd have better luck farther up the mountain. After another twisting mile he located an area alongside the road wide enough to park the car. He pulled off, cracked the windows a few inches and made sure the doors were locked, before slipping into his suit jacket to ward off the evening chill. Satisfied he wouldn't freeze to death, he stretched out in the passenger seat.

Night sounds filtered into the car. Strange, annoying

noises—scratching, owl hoots, creaking tree branches, moaning winds. Give him sirens, car alarms and diesel trucks any day.

As he drifted off to sleep, visions of Lightning Jack filled his mind. Call it reporter's intuition, but Sullivan's gut insisted the bootlegger hid nearby.

Chapter Two

"Explain to me again why we're running this man off?"

Jo scowled at her best friend, Annie McKee, then squirmed into a more comfortable position. "He's up to no good."

For the past fifteen minutes she and Annie had been hunkered down in the bushes, spying on the red Corvette. Thank goodness Betty Sue had phoned Jo to warn her that a stranger had dropped by the café asking questions about Lightning Jack. Jo hadn't been able to suppress the tiny thrill that had zipped through her at the news Sullivan Mooreland had returned. Then common sense kicked in and she attributed her foolish female reaction to a six-year dry spell without a man.

"What kind of no good?" Annie badgered.

"He's nosing around for information on Lightning Jack."

"Well, the guy can ask all he wants, that doesn't mean he'll get answers. I heard Lightning Jack has never been seen in person. Shoot, the old coot could have died years ago and no one in the clan would have known it."

What Annie said was true. The clan—save the elders—had no idea who Lightning Jack was and wouldn't be any help to the reporter, which made Jo feel even guiltier for secretly following in her deceased grandfather's footsteps the past two years. But what choice did she have? If anyone uncovered the truth, she'd lose her sole means of support for the school in the hollow.

"His name is Sullivan Mooreland and he intends to do a feature story about the bootlegger's activities. The clan doesn't need that kind of publicity."

"Shoot, Jo. Let the nosy reporter run loose in the hollow for a few days. If you're lucky he'll get lost on the mountain and you'll be rid of the problem."

She had to give the stranger credit—he was persistent if nothing else. If he intended to waltz back up the mountain without an invitation, he was in for a big surprise—the Heather's Hollow welcoming committee was like none other in existence. "Let's try to scare him off first. If it doesn't work, I'll figure out something else."

April's full moon, called the Pink Moon by locals, cast its iridescent glow across the patches of wild phlox blooming along the hillside, and enabled Jo and her coconspirator to view the trespasser sleeping inside the car.

"I'm too old for this," Annie grumbled.

"You, the queen of tree climbing, complaining about playing a little prank?" Jo snorted. "Remember the afternoon we caught old man Bundy washing his long johns in nothing but his birthday suit?"

"Yeah, I remember."

"He resembled a wild animal, with all that red fuzz covering his back and butt."

Annie sighed. She did that a lot lately—sigh. The *sighing* routine was what had prompted Jo to invite her childhood comrade along on tonight's escapade. The mother of twelve-year-old twin boys, Annie had her hands full raising her sons while her husband worked in the Blue Creek Coal Mine along the Virginia border a hundred miles east of Finnegan's Stand. Jo believed her friend could do with a thrill in her life.

"Did you drag me all the way out here to sit and watch the guy sleep?" Annie asked.

Now Jo wanted to sigh. "We have to scare him off."

"How?"

"With these." Jo dug into her pockets and produced two slingshots.

"Are you crazy? You can't shoot rocks at his car. He'll have you arrested for vandalism."

"Not rocks. Berries." Jo motioned to the American holly bushes a few yards behind them. "The birds haven't eaten all the winter berries."

"Berries won't scare the guy off."

Annie's grumpiness grated on Jo's nerves, but she held her tongue. Jo had heard through the grapevine that Annie and her husband argued the weekends he returned home from the mine. Jo assumed Sean was angry he'd been forced to take the mining job in order to save money for the boys' future education—an education he believed unnecessary. Annie, on the other hand, insisted she wanted better for the boys than a job in a mine or the sawmill in the hollow.

"He's a city slicker. He'll spook easily."

"And if he doesn't?" Annie asked.

"He will." Not at all confident the reporter would scatter, Jo added, "Make sure you hide in the shadows so he can't see us." Jo and Annie spent the next five minutes stuffing their pockets with red berries.

"You go for the open window. I'll hit the side of the car," Jo instructed.

They crouched, took aim and fired.

Ping, ping, ping.

"Maybe he's deaf." Annie let loose another round. "He's sitting up." A moment later they heard—

"Yeow!"

"I pegged him in the head," Annie squealed excitedly. "Chicken," she added when the car engine turned over and the window went up.

"He's leaving." As soon as the words exited Jo's mouth, the engine shut off.

"Guess not." Annie crawled off on her hands and knees to gather more ammunition.

"Keep pelting the car. He won't want his fancy Corvette messed with."

A few seconds after they unloaded another barrage of fruit bombs, the car door opened. *Oh, dear.* "Duck," Jo commanded, and they both dived behind a bush.

"Who the hell's out there?" he shouted. He must not have expected an answer, because he sprang out of the passenger seat, slammed the door shut, then raced around to the other side of the car and hid from sight.

Big chicken.

"Got a backup plan?" Annie whispered.

"Not really."

He raised his arm and Jo spotted something in his hand.

"I'm calling the police," he shouted over the hood of the car.

Jo and Annie exchanged grins. There was no cell-phone coverage in the area. *Ping, ping, ping.*

"That's it," he bellowed.

Jo grabbed Annie's wrist and tugged her farther into the shadows.

Sullivan Mooreland moved around the 'Vette and marched up the hillside.

Hell's bells! He was coming after them. "Keep shooting," she commanded.

Hands in front of his face, he growled like a bear roused from hibernation. Right when Jo figured their goose was cooked, he tripped and went down hard. She held her breath, waiting for him to rise. When he didn't, she worried that he might have been hurt.

"Wait—" Annie grasped Jo's arm when she attempted to stand "—he might be faking it."

"I don't think so." Jo set aside the slingshot and cautiously moved closer. After grabbing a stick from the ground, she poked his shoulder. No reaction. Maybe he was ticklish. She wiggled the tip of the stick inside his ear. Nothing.

"Is he dead?" Annie called from the bushes.

Dead? Good Lord, she hoped not. Jo's gaze zeroed in on his chest. "He's breathing." She dropped to her knees and ran her fingers through his hair, trying to ignore the silky feel of the strands as she searched for a wound. When she pressed against a lump, he groaned. "Yep, he hit his head and knocked himself out." She shook his shoulder. No response. "Sullivan, wake up."

"You two are on a first-name basis?" Annie grinned and plopped down next to Jo.

"This isn't funny." What had she done? Not only had she been dishonest with her fellow clan members, she'd caused bodily harm to a stranger. She never intended to carry on her illegal activities forever, but she'd yet to figure out a legitimate way to support the school. If some two-bit newspaper reporter exposed her, all her hard work would be for nothing. Worse, the children would lose their school.

"What now?" Annie nagged.

"We move him to my grandfather's fishing cabin."

Annie's eyes widened. "The cabin's a half mile away."

"You have a better idea?"

"Leave him for buzzard bait. That'll teach him to snoop around where he's not welcome."

"Why are you complaining? You've got plenty of practice dragging Sean's drunken hide home after he's been out on a bender," Jo accused.

"That was years ago. Now I just leave him to sleep it off wherever he passes out, usually in the woods behind the cabin."

"C'mon. Talking won't get the job done."

"You owe me big-time for this, Johanna Macpherson." Annie grunted.

"Remind me later." She and Annie shoved Sullivan to a sitting position, then hauled him to his feet. They each stuck a shoulder under an armpit and dragged him like a drunk sailor through the woods.

After a twenty-five-minute hike, they arrived at the cabin and got the reporter inside. "Hold him," Jo instructed. Annie plastered her hands against Sullivan's chest to keep him from sliding off the cane-back chair, while Jo confiscated a flashlight. She shined the beam on his face, then checked the bump on the side of his head.

"He's kind of handsome," Annie admitted.

"For shame, Annie. You're a married woman," Jo teased.

Snort. "Marriage isn't all it's cracked up to be." Annie grabbed the end of the rope Jo had fished from the storage chest in the corner.

Now wasn't the time to discuss Annie's marital problems, so Jo allowed the comment to pass by. They used a rolling-hitch knot to secure the flatlander, confident their prisoner wouldn't be going anywhere—at least not without the chair. *Now what?* Jo had to devise a new plan to encourage him to leave the hollow on his own. Frustrated, she grabbed a tin cup from the wooden shelf near the dry sink and left the cabin. A minute later, she returned with cool well water and placed the drink on the table next to the chair.

Annie rolled her eyes. "And how is he supposed to reach that all trussed up?"

"If he's thirsty enough, he'll figure out a way." At her friend's frown, Jo assured her, "Don't worry. Granny's baby-sitting Katie tonight. I'll stay here and keep an eye on him." Sullivan Mooreland would most certainly turn out to be the biggest pain in the rear. Why, then, did her chest tweak a bit at the sight of his drooping head? In his unconscious state he appeared innocent, with his light brown lashes sweeping his cheek, mouth relaxed and frown lines smoothed away.

As if her fingers had a will of their own, they brushed his mussed hair from his forehead, lingering a fraction of a second against the soft skin at his hairline. Jo jumped at the sound of Annie clearing her throat in the doorway. She'd been so caught up in studying Sullivan she'd forgotten all about her friend.

"Better watch yourself, Jo. That reporter may want more than a story from you." Annie slipped away into the night, leaving Jo alone with the man.

"If you know what's good for you, Sullivan Mooreland from Seattle, you'll tuck tail and run as far from this place as you can."

"PSST. MISTER, PSST."

In the far corners of his mind, Sullivan heard an insect buzzing. He fought to ignore the sound, but the insect grew hands and patted his knee, the touch more irritating than the *psst* sound. He swallowed—attempted to, rather. But with no saliva in his mouth, the sides of his throat stuck together. He opened one eye, then closed it when a bolt of bright light seared his retina. *Good God.* How much beer had he drunk last night?

After five seconds his numb brain challenged, *What beer?*

If he wasn't hungover, why did his head feel like a pumpkin that had been impaled on a picket-fence post? A constricting band compressed his chest, his numb arms tingled and his cell phone dug into his right butt cheek. What the hell had happened? The *pat, pat, pat* continued. "Stop," he begged.

"Mama says you have to eat," a voice insisted.

Red curls came into focus before his face. Lots of curls. Messy curls. Curls that belonged to a little girl with huge blue eyes and a freckled pixie face. *A fairy.* A wingless fairy, wearing jean overalls and a yellow T-shirt with a sparkly butterfly on the front. Tiny hands held a bowl.

Sullivan's stomach churned as he studied the contents. "You want me to eat mush?"

"It isn't mush." Her narrow chest puffed up.

In no shape to go a couple of rounds with a pint-sized spitfire, he stared in confusion at the rope across his chest, before he realized he was tied to a chair.

The events of the previous day flashed through Sullivan's mind—the Corvette running out of gas…his being chased by a pack of wild dogs…the woman with the floppy hat and grubby overalls giving him wrong directions…on purpose! Later that evening in the café the suspicious glances from Paul Bunyan's twin sister…his falling asleep along the side of the road. Then being awoken by pinging sounds hitting his car and discovering he was the target of an ambush.

The discomfort in his brain suggested he'd smacked his head when he'd fallen. Instead of fearing for his life, he felt a rush of excitement race through him, his pain temporarily forgotten. He must have stumbled—literally—into Lightning Jack's territory. He suspected the waitress at the café had sounded an alarm, warning the bootlegger that a stranger had been asking questions.

"Are you gonna eat, mister?" Big, blue, owl eyes blinked.

"I'm not hungry," he protested. "What's your name?"

"Katie. Mama said my papaw used to call me Katie lady."

"How old are you?"

"Six." Her chin rose in the air, as if she was daring him to think her younger. She seemed too tiny to be a six-year-old. Then again, what did he know about kids?

"Mama says I'm her little leprechaun."

God help him. He'd fallen through the rabbit hole into the land of make-believe. Of course the child was pulling his leg, but just in case… "Do you have magical powers?"

Red corkscrew curls boinged against her shoulders when she shook her head. "But I can whistle real good." She rested the bowl on Sullivan's lap, then stuck two fingers in her mouth and let out a shrill sound that threatened to split his head in two.

He opened his mouth to shout *Stop*, but the freckle-faced imp's sweet smile reached inside his chest and squeezed his heart. How could he yell at such a cute…leprechaun? His stomach rumbled reminding him that his last meal had been a slice of apple pie. One bite wouldn't hurt. "If I eat, will you be quiet?"

With a solemn face, she held up the spoon.

The tasty bacon-and-ham-flavor surprised Sullivan and he allowed her to shovel another glob into his mouth.

"Did your father tie me up?" The spoon paused above the bowl.

"I don't have a daddy. But my friend Sarah has two." She tilted her head to the side. "Do you have a daddy?"

"No," Sullivan growled. Then regretted his harsh response when the girl jumped. In a calmer voice, he explained, "I never knew my father."

"Mama says it's okay if I don't have a daddy 'cause she loves me twice as much."

Sullivan hurt for the kid. He'd always believed he'd been better off without a father than having one who didn't want to be a father—unless girls were different from boys and required more security. He shook his head. Why did he care if the munchkin was fatherless? "Where's your mother?" His talent lay in asking questions, not analyzing kids' feelings.

"Teaching."

"Teaching what?"

"School, silly." She giggled—a light tinkling sound that made Sullivan smile.

Interesting. A schoolteacher. "Did your mother bring me to this cabin?"

Narrow shoulders shrugged, then she offered another spoonful of gunk and asked, "Is your mama a teacher, too?"

"No, she's dead."

Blue eyes widened. "Did you cry?"

Cry when his alcoholic mother had finally succumbed to cirrhosis of the liver? *No.* "A little," he lied.

"What's your job?"

"I'm a reporter."

"What's a reporter?"

"A person who writes stories for a newspaper."

"We don't read newspapers, but my mamaw left my mama lots of books before she died."

"What's a mamaw?"

"A mamaw's a mamaw, silly."

"Your grandmother?" he guessed.

"Uh-huh."

Sullivan checked the bowl, surprised he'd eaten more than half the contents. "What's the name of your school?"

Brownish red eyebrows dipped over her pug nose. "It doesn't have a name."

"Where is it?" Any tidbit of information might prove helpful in his search for Lightning Jack.

She pointed the spoon at the cabin window. "Thatta way."

"Why aren't you in school?"

"'Cause the older kids have to take tests."

"Tests for what?"

"High school. Did you go to high school?"

"Yes, I did."

"Where?"

"In the state of Washington. Far away from here."

Her mouth formed an O.

"What do you do when you're not in school?" he asked.

"I jump rope with Sarah. And I help Mama cook. Sometimes I help Granny pick flowers and dig up roots. She makes lots of medicines from 'em."

"Is Granny your grandmother?"

"No, but Granny babysits me. And she fixes people when they get sick."

Granny sounded like a witch doctor. Before he had the chance to ask exactly how the old woman fixed people, Sullivan's cell phone rang—the theme of "Hey, Hey, We're the Monkeys." He rolled onto one butt cheek and the phone cut off.

The little girl held a hand over her mouth and giggled. "Your pants can sing, mister."

Oh, no. His trousers were about to do more than sing… they were going to whistle. "Hey, kid. Untie me. I need to use the bathroom."

"Mama said all I can do is feed you."

Mama must have doctored up the mush, because Sullivan's bowels were on the verge of howling. "Go get your mother. Hurry. It's an emergency."

The elf sniffed the air and pinched the end of her nose. "Yuck!" she shouted, then dashed out the cabin door. Sullivan wasn't sure how long he could hang on before breakfast exploded from him.

Less than a minute passed before the little girl burst into the cabin, tugging the hand of a woman. "He's got the trots, Mama."

For a moment Sullivan forgot his discomfort. *Mama* was the same woman who'd rescued him from the pack of hunting dogs, then sent him off in the wrong direction. And he had a sneaking suspicion she'd been the one hiding in the woods, shooting berries at his car last night.

Similar to her daughter, Mama possessed a mass of untamed red curls and bright blue eyes, which glinted with humor. Dressed the way she was in slim-fitting jeans and a plain T-shirt, her curves stood out in plain view—not concealed beneath baggy overalls as they had been yesterday. If his intestines weren't in such pain, he'd give those curves the inspection they deserved. When her gaze landed on the almost-empty bowl, he accused, "You put something in that cr—" He caught the worried expression on the little girl's face, then amended, "That *stuff.*"

"A secret ingredient to keep you from wandering off too far." Her eyes twinkled as she moved forward to untie him.

"Better plug your nose, Mama," Katie warned.

Sullivan's face heated. He didn't make a habit of passing gas in front of women—even beautiful, spiteful women such as the one unbinding him. His stomach spasmed and sweat broke out across his brow as he fought to keep from breaking wind. *Hurry.* He glanced about the one-room shack. "Where's the bathroom?"

"The outhouse is around back."

An outhouse—though right now a bush would do. As soon as the last knot loosened, he bolted from the chair, then fell flat on his face when his numb legs gave out. The woman bent to help him, but he waved her off. He stumbled to his feet, then wobbled out the door. Ignoring the pinpricking pain in his legs, he dashed around the side of the cabin and spotted the latrine—at the top of the hill twenty yards away.

He sprinted across the open space, unbuckling his belt and unzipping his pants as he ran. When he yanked open the outhouse door, something scampered across the top of one shoe, but he paid no attention. He dropped his drawers and squatted over the larger of the two holes in the wooden bench.

The blue sky peeked through the crescent moon carved into

the door, as Sullivan wondered what the heck he'd done to deserve a butt full of splinters and a beautiful redhead hell-bent on running him out of Heather's Hollow.

Chapter Three

Jo tamped her foot against the ground. Sullivan Mooreland from Seattle had been in the Thunder Box, as her grandfather had called it, for almost an hour. Obviously city folk, with their weak intestines, were no match for Granny O'Neil's stool mover.

The outhouse dated back to 1920 and listed dangerously to the right. If she was lucky, the crapper would collapse and she'd be done with the reporter. "You coming out any time soon?"

"Where's the toilet paper?" he shouted. "Or should I be searching for a Sears Roebuck catalog?"

Smart-ass.

"You still there?" he called through the moon in the door.

What a nuisance. "Check the coffee can." Jo had been taught by her mother to put a roll of toilet paper inside a coffee can with a handful of rice. The rice absorbed the moisture and kept the paper fresh. The last time she'd used her grandfather's outhouse had been over two years ago. No telling if there was tissue in the can or not. For all she cared, the nosy stranger could wipe his backside with the sole of his shoe.

"Found it!"

Frustrated, she paced, hating that she'd had to dismiss her

students early when they'd been in the middle of exams. Although not mandatory, Jo administered state tests once a year. Often her students scored higher than those attending the school in Finnegan's Stand. Because Jo didn't teach a state-approved curriculum, Kentucky law considered the school in the hollow private, therefore it was exempt from rigorous government regulations. Each year, Jo was asked to send a letter listing the names and residences of the students enrolled in the school. As long as she kept attendance records, made sure the kids received a hundred and seventy-five days of instruction and she turned in regular scholarship reports, approval of her curriculum from the public-school district wasn't required.

The outhouse door creaked. *Finally.* She'd seen sheep less sheepish-looking than the reporter. Pale and hunched, he appeared downright miserable. A tiny sliver of empathy stabbed Jo, but she straightened her shoulders and ignored the sensation. The man was trouble. The sooner she ran him off, the better.

Shuffling to within a foot of her, he stopped, his hawkish features more pronounced because of the pinched expression on his face. Instead of feeling threatened by his proximity, her skin prickled with awareness, and she found it impossible to drag her attention from the firm line of his sexy mouth.

"What exactly did you put in that food your kid fed me?" he demanded.

"Buckthorn bark, psyllium husk, anise seed, fennel seed—"

He raised a hand, ending her recitation of ingredients. "That was you in the woods last night, pelting my car with berries, wasn't it?"

Blast! She'd hoped the knock on his skull would have clouded his memory. "I don't know what you're talking about."

He nuzzled her neck, and she jumped back in surprise. "Yep, I remember that smell."

"What smell?" He'd just sniffed her like a dog. And

truth be told, she rather liked the feel of his big nose nudging her neck.

When he lowered his head again, she forced herself to stand still. "Last night I caught a whiff of something citrusy. You."

Being compared to a fruit was hardly complimentary. However, her ego appreciated that after clunking his head, the only thing he recalled was her scent.

He crossed his arms over his chest. "Care to explain why you abducted me?"

Abducted? That was a bit far-fetched. "I found you lying on the ground, unconscious. The cabin was close by. I brought you here to…to recover."

"And tied me to a chair?"

"I didn't want you to fall and hit your head again." That sounded reasonable, didn't it?

"Your concern for my well-being led you to poison me?"

After this interrogation, she decided she should have taken her chances and left Sullivan Mooreland alongside the road, instead of going on the attack with a slingshot. "If you woke and decided to search for your car, you might have gotten lost in the woods."

A stretch of silence followed her statement and she resisted the urge to squirm under his stare. She wondered if the color of his eyes intensified during…*good grief.* What in tarnation was wrong with her? She must be suffering from some kind of horny spell.

"You're afraid," he accused.

"Afraid of what?"

"That I'll find Lightning Jack."

Whenever she heard the bootlegger's name, Jo's chin raised a notch.

"I knew it," he gloated. "The outlaw's around here somewhere, isn't he?"

"You should leave. You're not welcome here."

"If I'm not welcome, then why the hell did you take me hostage?"

Because I panicked! Isn't it bad enough, Jo, that you're breaking the law to fund the school? Did you have to accost a stranger, too? Thank goodness her mother wasn't alive to witness this episode of temporary insanity. "I'm sorry about all that. I'll be happy to escort you back to—"

"I'm not leaving."

Jo admired the reporter's boldness in standing up to her. She had a reputation for being bullheaded, and most men steered clear of her—not that she'd been approached by many men over the years.

If truth be told, there were few eligible males of marrying age in the clan and they weren't very exciting. To her chagrin, she admitted she wanted more from a husband than a roof over her head and food on the table. She already provided those things for herself and Katie. Aside from the obvious physical intimacy that came with marriage, she yearned for intellectual stimulation from her mate—something she suspected the hothead glaring at her would be full of. She opened her mouth to remind him that he was trespassing, but his question caught her by surprise.

"Where's my Corvette?"

"The car's stowed in a safe place." At least she'd been considerate enough to retrieve his overnight bag and toiletry kit from the vehicle.

The flatlander growled. He stormed several feet away, then swung around. "I've been up front with you from the beginning. I told you the truth about why I'm here. You're the one who's lied, tricked and poisoned me."

Okay, now he was making her feel like the stuff at the bottom of the crapper.

"Well?" Brown eyebrows arched.

"Well, what?"

"Don't I deserve an apology?"

Apologize? The man was insane on top of being too darned handsome for his own good. "If I say I'm sorry, will you leave?"

"Hell, no," he snapped.

"You're not going to locate Lightning Jack." That was the God's honest truth.

"Then there should be no problem if I snoop around. Once I'm convinced the bootlegger isn't here, I'll leave."

"Mister—"

"Sullivan. I don't believe I caught your name."

Because I never tossed it your way. "Johanna Macpherson. I go by Jo."

"A few days, then I'm as good as gone. What do you say, Johanna?" Her name trickled off his tongue—the smooth, silky sound similar to running creek water over sandstone. Her track record with men—make that a man—insisted that keeping her guard up around the reporter would be difficult if not impossible.

She considered allowing him to remain in the hollow. If Sullivan Mooreland believed he'd find a local willing to spill his or her guts, he was mistaken. Sullivan could ask questions until he turned blue in the face, only to receive an answer that made no sense.

"You've got three days." Even though she admired his tenacity, and admitted she found him intriguing and wished to become better acquainted with him, she hated that she'd lost the first round to the flatlander.

"That should be plenty of time to get my story. Is there a motel nearby?"

Well, shoot. She hadn't considered where he'd sleep. Best he hang his hat with her—easier to keep an eye on him, she told herself. "You can bunk at my place."

"I'll pay for food and lodging."

"It's an insult for a guest, even an unwanted one, to pay." She walked off, then paused when she noticed he hadn't followed. A glance over her shoulder confirmed her suspicion— Sullivan Mooreland was sprinting to the Thunder Box.

This was going to be a long day.

LEERY OF Johanna Macpherson's invitation to stay at her home, Sullivan trudged behind mother and daughter along a trail that supposedly led to Jo's truck. "Why aren't there more roads up here?"

No answer, but he caught the stiffening of her shoulders— *again*. What did she expect from a reporter? Inquisitiveness was in his genes. Too bad the hollow was a sensitive subject with his host, because he had a million questions he craved answers to. He gave up on the questions and concentrated on the view in front of him—the sexy sway of Jo's jean-clad hips. Normally he was attracted to women who wore high heels and tight business suits with skirts that ended at mid-thigh. He'd never thought girl-next-door attire sexy. Then again, he'd never seen a girl-next-door quite like Johanna Macpherson. Her fiery-red curls matched her personality and the thought of going head to head with the spirited woman excited him.

Five more minutes passed and he spotted the beat-up truck. *Thank God*. Light-headed and dehydrated from battling his bowels, Sullivan was on the verge of collapse. "Got any water? Or soda?"

"Mama won't buy pop 'cause it's bad for my teeth," the little twerp explained. At least the daughter submitted more than yes-or-no answers, unlike her mother.

Well, hell. A lack-of-caffeine-induced migraine couldn't be half as painful as having his entrails cleaned out.

"You'll have to wait for a drink until we reach the house." Jo opened the truck door and the child hopped in.

The drive was made in silence. Twice, Curly Top peeked up at him, but he kept his gaze straight ahead. He wasn't in the mood for senseless kid chatter. His first glimpse of Jo's home reminded him of a circa 1800 photograph. The bleached-poplar logs didn't detract from its well-built and maintained appearance. A fieldstone foundation supported the boxy structure made of twenty-five- to thirty-five-foot long logs. Clay chinking had been used to seal the gaps between the logs. Weathered shake shingles composed the roof and a stone chimney braced one end of the structure.

An overhang supported by three sturdy posts ran across the front of the house, creating a covered porch. Pots of flowers decorated the steps, and two rocking chairs and a handmade three-legged table rested in front of a large picture window. Above the porch overhang was a second story, with two narrower size windows trimmed in red to match the front door. A smaller structure with a crumbled chimney occupied the yard to the right of the main cabin. Probably a cookhouse at one time.

"Where's the outhouse?" he asked.

Jo parked near a lean-to and helped her daughter from the truck, then explained. "This was my grandparents' cabin. My grandfather had indoor plumbing installed as a gift to my grandmother for her fiftieth birthday."

Imagine that. No woman Sullivan had ever dated would have been thrilled to receive a toilet for a birthday gift. Strung across the tops of the trees, was a power line, which connected to a junction box at the side of the house. Taking advantage of his hostess's sudden verbosity, he asked, "What about electricity?"

"Most homes have electricity now," Jo answered. "But some of the older folks prefer the outhouse to indoor plumbing."

Sullivan would trade electricity for a toilet any day. He followed the females into the cabin, then stopped in the doorway to study the interior. A wide-plank floor covered the first level, which was split in half by a staircase leading to the second story. The kitchen was located to one side, the family room to the other.

"Bathroom's behind the stairs. Water's in the fridge." Jo glared.

"Don't worry." Hands in the air, he promised, "I won't run off with the silver."

While Jo went upstairs to check on her daughter, he used the time to explore the bathroom. A huge claw-foot tub graced the center of the room. A small window next to the tub presented the bather with an authentic Appalachian view—magnificent vistas dotted with flowering dogwoods against a hazy blue sky. A pedestal sink stood across from the tub and an old-fashioned toilet with a pull chain completed the necessary items in the room. Unable to resist, he tugged the chain and grinned when the water whooshed down the toilet.

The room wasn't filled with knickknacks, which appealed to Sullivan. Rust-colored towels hung from an iron rod behind the tub, and a hook on the back of the door held a green bathrobe. The bar of soap on the sink had flower petals pressed into it—probably homemade.

Next, he checked out the kitchen. An electric stove was shoved against the far wall. A few feet away stood a refrigerator, small in comparison with the ones manufactured today. A microwave occupied one end of the counter and a coffeemaker, the other. There was a glass-paned door in the far corner that led to a screened-in porch. He wasn't sure what he expected when he peeked inside the refrigerator, but it hadn't been cartoon-character yogurt, packaged string cheese and juice boxes. Johanna Macpherson was an intriguing blend of old and new. He grabbed a water bottle and chugged.

A sofa, recliner and a coffee table sat on the colorful braided rug in the family room. A sewing basket rested on the sofa cushion. The stone fireplace comprised the far wall. Hooks had been drilled into the mortar along the front of the mantel to hang copper pots and kettles. The simple decor was cozy, warm and welcoming.

"I'm sure it's not what you're used to." Jo stood on the bottom stair.

The comment startled him. "You don't know anything about me or what I'm used to."

Ignoring his assertion, she retreated to the kitchen, fussed with the dial on the oven, then retrieved a pan of rolls from the porch and slipped it into the oven.

Light footsteps on the stairs reminded him that he and Jo weren't alone. "Hi, again, mister."

"Ah, the little leprechaun." Sullivan smiled and was rewarded with a high-pitched giggle. He switched his attention to the leprechaun's mother, who had placed a black kettle on the stove.

"Katie, set the table," Jo instructed.

The imp obeyed, digging silverware out of a drawer. Feeling useless, he asked, "What can I do?"

"We're having leftover stew." Jo nodded to the glass-fronted cupboards.

Stew meant bowls. He selected three blue-and-beige pottery dishes that looked handmade. "Have you always lived in the hollow?" He arranged the bowls on the table.

"Born and raised and planning on—" she glanced at her daughter "—retiring here." A comfortable silence filled the kitchen for the next few minutes, then the oven timer dinged. "Katie, honey, will you get the rolls?"

Sullivan beat the child across the room. "Let me." He had no experience with kids, but wasn't a six-year-old too young to be sticking her hands inside an oven?

The leprechaun stamped her foot. "I can do it, mister."

"You might burn your hands or catch your hair on fire." He glanced at the mother for help, but Mama remained silent.

"I'm a big girl," Katie argued.

Hovering, he watched the child slide her hands into mitts that ended at her armpits. She opened the oven door and reached in from the side to remove the pan, then slid it onto the counter before closing the door and flipping the dial to Off.

"I'm impressed," he complimented her.

Katie smiled. "Told ya so."

"Braggy-puss," he grouched.

Throaty, warm laughter met Sullivan's ears and he found himself wanting to make Jo laugh again. "She takes after her mother, I see." No laughter this time, only a wide smile—reward enough. Johanna's smile was a breathtaking sight. *Steady, ol' boy. You're here for a story. Nothing more.* But if he wanted more…the woman with the flaming head of hair would be at the top of his list.

"If you haven't already puzzled it out for yourself, you'll learn soon enough that the Scotch-Irish clan of Heather's Hollow is fiercely independent."

As if to prove her mother's words, Katie dragged a chair to the counter and climbed up so she could place the rolls in a basket, which she then delivered to the table. "So I'm learning," Sullivan conceded.

After ladling stew into the three bowels, Jo seated herself.

Stomach grumbling at the yeasty smell of fresh-baked bread, he lifted his butter knife and reached for a roll.

"Wait, mister. We have to thank God for our food."

"Sorry," he muttered.

"Mama says guests get to say grace." Katie grasped his hand, while Jo clasped his other.

The feel of such small fingers in one of his hands made Sullivan realize how vulnerable children were. In his other hand…the feel of Jo's slightly callused fingers made him think of…*sex.*

"Dear God, help me—I mean, thank you for this food. Amen."

Jo couldn't escape his grasp fast enough, but Katie held on and squeezed. "You done good, mister," she praised him.

The aroma of stew and bread was lethal to a starving man. He was so hungry his stomach gnawed his backbone, yet his spoon hovered in front of his mouth. *What if…*

"I didn't poison the food." As if to prove her point, Jo swallowed a bite. "Pass the bread to Mr. Mooreland, Katie."

"She can call me Sullivan."

"No, she can't. It's not respectful or polite."

He made a silly face and Katie giggled, slapping a hand over her mouth before staring wide-eyed at her mother.

What had gotten into him, goofing off with a kid? "How about calling me Mr. Sully?"

Katie glanced at her mother. "Mama?"

"As long as I hear the Mr.—" Jo's voice lowered to a whisper "—you can call him anything you want."

Ha, ha. Sullivan stuffed his mouth with stew meat to keep from grinning. They ate in silence for a few minutes, and when he was confident his intestines weren't going to rebel, he praised, "This tastes great."

"Thanks."

"Katie said you were a teacher."

"I have twenty-three students between the ages of six and thirteen."

"Don't tell me you teach in a one-room schoolhouse."

"Mama has a pretty school," Katie interjected.

"Thank you, sweetie." Jo patted her daughter's hand, then swung her gaze to Sullivan. "This spring, we put a fresh coat of white paint on the building. And to answer your question, it's a two-room schoolhouse. There's a small bathroom inside."

"Why aren't the kids attending school in Finnegan's Stand?"

"The public curriculum glosses over Appalachian history."

"Finnegan's Stand is part of the Appalachian Mountains. Wouldn't they teach the area's history?"

"They cover the history, but they don't address the *problems* facing those living in this part of the country today."

Her eyes flashed and the blaze of pink across her cheeks distracted him. Maybe it was a trick of the light, but he swore her red hair crackled. Her enthusiasm for education fascinated him.

"Each year Appalachian communities lose more and more young adults to the cities. Take our clan, for instance." She tore off a piece of roll and stuffed it into her mouth. "There are sixty-two extended families living in the hollow. Total population— 372. Over the past five years, twenty-seven young adults have left to attend college or seek higher-paying jobs."

"You went away to college to earn a teaching degree. What made you decide to return?" he asked, enjoying the rarity of having a civil conversation with the woman.

"When I arrived at the University of Kentucky in Lexington, the chain restaurants, retail stores, movie theaters and the huge number of young people my own age impressed me." She paused as if she'd caught herself before divulging a secret, the she dropped her gaze and chased a piece of stew meat with her spoon. "I discovered the city wasn't all it was cracked up to be."

Sullivan suspected something—or rather, *someone*—had happened to Jo to send her scurrying back to the hollow. His interest in the area and Jo's passion for the subject compelled him to press on. "And you believe teaching Appalachian history will encourage the younger generation to stick around?"

"After I graduated from college, I landed a teaching job in Finnegan's Stand. My first year there I attempted to organize a career day at the elementary school and was shocked when my fifth-graders vehemently protested."

"Why?"

"The kids were embarrassed by their parents. Embarrassed by who they were." She shook her head. "Said things like, 'What's so cool about sawing down a bunch of trees?' Or, 'All my mom does is stand in front of a conveyer belt and stick labels on cans.' And, 'My dad works in a coal mine. He'd just get the place dirty.'"

"Most kids are self-conscious about their moms and dads." Hell, he'd been more times than he could count—his mother showing up drunk for a teacher conference. Volunteering for a PTO fund-raiser, then sending packaged cookies from the Dollar Store, instead of homemade ones.

"I decided that the only way to instill a sense of pride in the younger generation was to not only teach the history of the area but to explain the problems facing our unique culture. I spent hours and hours creating a curriculum."

After a lengthy silence, he prompted, "And…"

"And the school board shot it down. They argued they wanted kids to better themselves, not stay the same." Jo carried her empty bowl to the sink. "That's when I realized even the adults in the community were ashamed of their roots. I resigned my teaching position and presented my curriculum to the clan elders. They supported me wholeheartedly and we built a school in the hollow."

"Impressive," he admitted. Sullivan couldn't remember the last time he'd reported on a story with such fervor, such conviction. Jo's enthusiasm fueled his own, making him more determined to find Lightning Jack. "Any chance you can arrange for me to meet these esteemed elders you speak of?"

"We'll see," she hedged. "While I'm at the school, you'll have to remain at the cabin."

And do what? Twiddle his thumbs?

Katie slid off the chair and carried her bowl to the sink, then retrieved Sullivan's. He would have offered to clean up, but scraping, rinsing and washing dishes was more involved than dumping fast-food containers into a garbage can.

"How about if I tag along with you to school tomorrow," he proposed.

"No, the kids are testing." Jo placed a mug of coffee in front of him. He sipped the hot brew and grimaced. Maybe by the time he left the hollow he'd have acquired a taste for the nasty bean. "Anything need fixing around the place?" Not that he'd be much help. When something broke in his apartment, he slipped a note under the manager's door and a handyman showed up the next day.

"Nothing's broken." Jo scowled. "And don't wander off. A bear and her two cubs have been sighted three times near the hollow this spring. I'd hate to find your mauled carcass strewn about the yard."

Bear? That nixed his idea of exploring the woods around the cabin. As the two redheads puttered in the kitchen, he couldn't help but appreciate the cozy picture they made. Side by side, sharing a smile and an occasional laugh.

"Where's Mr. Macpherson?" The question slipped out before Sullivan could snatch it back.

"I'm not married." Jo's answer was devoid of emotion—*interesting.*

"Remember, Mr. Sully. I told you I don't have a daddy," Katie added.

"Katie pie, don't forget to feed Jelly."

Evidently the *daddy* topic remained off-limits. Sullivan's gaze followed the child. "Who's Jelly?"

"You'll see." Katie stopped at the screen door and whistled the same shrill sound that had threatened to burst Sullivan's eardrums that morning. Seconds later a huge Saint Bernard bounced up the porch steps and skidded to a halt. *Woof.*

"Jelly can't sleep in the house 'cept when it's real cold," Katie said. She scooped dog food from a bin by the door into a big plastic bowl, then stepped outside and set it down. She hugged the dog's neck and Jelly waited patiently until his owner finished loving him before he attacked the food.

The little girl stayed at Jelly's side, one small hand resting on the dog's back. While the child was preoccupied, Sullivan went fishing for details. "What happened to Katie's father?"

"None of your business."

Her abrupt answer stung. Feeling defensive, he muttered, "I never knew my father."

"What happened to yours?" Her cheeks pinkened, then she mumbled, "Never mind."

He'd never spoken about his past, not even to his fellow reporters. What was it about Johanna Macpherson that made him think she'd care about his childhood? "My mother didn't marry my father and she never talked about him. The first time I asked where he was, she cuffed me across the mouth and told me never to speak his name."

The pity in Jo's eyes made him uncomfortable. He should have kept his mouth shut.

"Things didn't work out between me and Katie's father," she added after a lengthy silence.

"Is he a member of the clan?"

She shook her head. "I met him in college."

"But he knows about Katie?" Sullivan wasn't sure what prompted the question. After Jo's impassioned speech about teaching kids to be proud of who they were, he doubted she'd keep Katie a secret from her father.

"Brian knows. He chooses not to have anything to do with her."

"That's rough. I remember wanting a father real bad when I was Katie's age."

"My daughter has plenty of men in her life."

"You mean, grandfathers and uncles."

"I'm an only child. My folks died in a car accident after I went away to college. My grandfather passed away a couple of years ago."

Jo was alone in the world, too. The commonalities between them intrigued Sullivan. "I'm sorry about your parents."

She flashed a sad smile. "The fathers in the clan include Katie in the activities they do with their own kids. We're a close-knit group."

The close-knit-group theory sounded nice, but Sullivan suspected the clan might be smothering at times.

"Jelly's done," Katie announced, her lips smashed against the screen door.

"Come inside and get ready for bed," Jo ordered.

Katie brought the dog dish to the sink, then paused at Sullivan's side. "'Night, Mr. Sully."

"Sweet dreams, little leprechaun."

The kid giggled all the way up the stairs.

Jo asked, "Ready to make up your bed?"

He eyed the short couch.

"Oh, no," she warned.

"Oh, no, what?"

"You're not sleeping in the house." Her hands clenched into fists as if ready to do battle.

"You're kicking me outside? What about the wild bear roaming the area?"

"The bear won't bother you in the cookhouse."

The cookhouse? "Thanks, but no, thanks. I'll sleep in my car again." At least he could drive off if the bear happened by.

"It's too late to retrieve the car."

"Where is it?"

"Don't worry. Your precious hotrod is safe and sound."

Unbelievable. "You orchestrated this, didn't you?" he accused.

"Orchestrated what?"

"Stranding me here." He feigned outrage, hoping she'd feel bad and change her mind about helping him locate Lightning Jack.

Fat chance. She snagged the afghan from the back of the couch and one of the throw pillows. "Don't stray too far from the cabin," she warned, shoving the bedding into his arms.

"If I do?" he challenged.

Her eyes twinkled. "Jeb's hounds will sniff you out of the woods."

"I'm guessing the cookhouse is that shack with the crumbling chimney."

"There's a candle and matches inside."

"What about a bed?"

"You'll have to make do with the table."

Swallowing a curse, he stepped outside and allowed his eyes to adjust to the dark. He scanned the woods surrounding the cabin and exhaled in relief when no glowing eyes watched from the underbrush. "Want to keep me company tonight, Jelly?" The dog's tail wagged.

"Scared of the boogeyman?" Jo teased, leaning a shoulder against the doorjamb.

Sullivan Mooreland scared?

"C'mon, Jelly." He snapped his fingers and the dog loped after him. Hell, yes, he was scared! No telling what kind of creatures lurked in these mountains at night.

Chapter Four

The illuminated numbers on the clock next to Jo's bed flipped to 12:00. *Midnight.* And she'd yet to fall asleep. Her conversation with Sullivan about Appalachian culture and the school in the hollow replayed in her mind. Ever since she'd quit her teaching job in Finnegan's Stand, she'd worried over whether the decision had been the right one for her and Katie. She'd walked away from a retirement fund, healthcare insurance, sick pay and other benefits.

Jo left the bed and stood sentry at the upstairs window, her gaze glued to the cookhouse across the yard. She wasn't sure why she'd kept the front-porch light on. To guarantee she'd spot Sullivan if he attempted to flee or because she felt sorry for him alone out there in the dark?

She closed her eyes and imagined the night sounds of a large city like Seattle. Sirens. Car alarms. Horn blasts. Life Flight helicopters and gunshots. Different from the noises in the hollow—nonstop cricket chirping, the *hoo, hoo, too-hoo* of the barred owl and the hiss of quarrelsome raccoons scuffling like angry cats.

Not for a minute did she believe Sullivan was stupid enough to traipse through the woods at night, searching for Lightning Jack. And since the truck keys sat on the kitchen counter downstairs, she trusted that Sullivan would stay put. Tomorrow was another story.

That he'd attempted to sneak back into the hollow after she'd shooed him away had left her no choice but to allow him in—if only to monitor his comings and goings. She didn't dare leave him unsupervised while she administered final exams tomorrow; no telling what kind of trouble he'd stir up. She had to seek help from the clan elders.

Quietly she shimmied out of her nightshirt and into a pair of athletic pants and a sweat jacket, then crept downstairs and shoved her feet into the sneakers by the front door. After slipping from the house, she bolted the lock, then crossed the yard to the guest chambers. Sullivan had left the door cracked.

When she poked her head inside, Jelly's ears perked. Jo raised her hand and the dog understood to stay. Sullivan lay on his stomach, sprawled across the wooden table in the center of the structure. His sock feet hung off the end and one hand rested on top of Jelly's fur—Jo suspected to keep the dog from running off in the middle of the night.

Big 'fraidy cat.

Soft moon glow seeped through the window beside the collapsed fireplace, illuminating his face. In sleep, his features appeared boyish. Quiet snores escaped his mouth. He'd been through hell's forty acres the past two days, and he'd still remained pleasant around her and Katie—except for telling her, *You don't know anything about me or what I'm used to.*

His defensive statement had taken Jo by surprise and had made her feel small. She despised others judging her and her way of life, but that was exactly what she'd done to Sullivan. Because he drove a car that cost more than her yearly income, she'd assumed he was rich and lived a privileged life. Yet, his voice had been filled with genuine warmth and honesty when he'd commented that her cabin felt homey. His approval had weakened her resistance against him and she'd ended up confessing private details about Katie's father that were none of Sullivan's business.

Sullivan Mooreland was a reporter on a mission. In three days he'd be gone. Back to Seattle. Back to his own life. Leaving her behind in the hollow. She rubbed her breastbone, wondering at the strange ache in her chest.

First things first. "Watch Katie, Jelly," she reiterated in a hushed voice. The dog would guard the house and attack anyone dumb enough to try to harm her daughter. Jo took the path that led to the heather fields and Granny O'Neil, the clan matriarch and healer. Tall trees blocked the bright moonlight, but she'd grown up running these trails and could navigate them with her eyes closed. The chilly night air made her shiver and she jogged to keep warm. She wasn't one to exercise regularly. Didn't have to.

Most days she and Katie walked to the school and at night she trekked through the woods to check the still her grandfather had used to manufacture heather whiskey. Her grandfather had allowed others in the clan to assume he made the whiskey for personal consumption. Only the elders knew he'd produced moonshine on a much larger scale and had sold it illegally, using the funds to pay for Jo's college tuition and to help other clan members in need. And some of that money had gone to build Jo's school.

Jo's grandfather held a special place in her heart. He'd been a solid shoulder to lean on after her parents' deaths. And when she'd returned to the hollow pregnant and disillusioned about love, he hadn't judged her. Instead he'd welcomed her home and had cherished Katie the moment she'd been born and he'd held his great-granddaughter in his arms.

When her grandfather had insisted she learn how to brew the clan's secret recipe for heather whiskey, Jo hadn't been able to say no. At the time, she'd believed she was honoring a clan tradition. She'd never expected to get caught up in the illegal manufacturing and selling of moonshine or to have to rely on the profits to support her school. The school meant the world to Jo, the future to the clan. If there were any other way to acquire funding, she'd shut down the still. Contrary to what a flatlander might believe, Jo did not enjoy breaking the law. She spent many restless nights worrying over what would happen to her daughter if Jo got apprehended by the sheriff.

After Jo had jogged fifteen minutes, the heather fields came into view. Skirting the edge of them, she approached Granny's cabin. As soon as Jo raised her hand to knock, old woman's ragged voice called out, "C'mon in."

Jo entered and closed the door, shutting out the damp night air.

"Been expectin' ya." Granny stirred a caramel-colored liquid in the iron cauldron hanging from a rod in the fireplace. Her stark white ponytail swayed against her black shawl.

The residents of Finnegan's Stand gossiped behind Granny's back, calling her names—mostly *witch*. Granny didn't cast spells, but once in a while she'd "see" with her mind—such as knowing Jo intended to visit tonight. The sight in their clan skipped a generation. Granny had discovered her uniqueness from her grandmother, not her mother. Since Granny's only child, Catherine, had run off years ago, the clan would never learn if the gift had been passed on. The elders credited Granny's "visions" for keeping the clan safe over the years. The younger generation insisted the old woman was batty.

"Don't you ever relax, Granny?" Jo asked.

"I'll git plenty of rest when I get to heaven." Nodding to the rocking chair in the corner of the one-room cabin, she instructed, "Sit."

Glad for the chance to catch her breath, Jo collapsed on the seat. Granny's cabin was one of two remaining structures dating back to the 1840s. Jo imagined Sullivan would be interested in viewing Granny's home and her Aunt Susan—the rickety outhouse in the backyard.

Granny sorted through the collection of bottles filling the shelves of a medicine cabinet her deceased husband had built shortly after they'd married. The piece of furniture resembled something out of an eighteenth-century apothecary shop, complete with row after row of numbered drawers. Drawer #15 hid sassafras, Granny's favorite remedy for colds. Dandelion, used as a diuretic, filled drawer #27, and #6 contained Virginia snakeroot, a gastric stimulant. The shelves held threadbare, leather-bound medical journals containing recipes for salves and medicines passed down through generations of Scottish healers. And along the top of the cabinet—jars of leeches. *Yuck.*

"Did he say what he wants?"

"Yes." Jo didn't understand why Granny had voiced the question when she probably realized Sullivan's reason for being here—unless…Granny couldn't "see" Sullivan's purpose in the hollow. The past few years the old woman had complained that the older she got, the less her mind "saw."

"Laws a-mighty, must be somethin' powerful bad to bring ya here in the middle of the night."

"His name's Sullivan Mooreland. He's a newspaper reporter from Seattle."

"Lookin' fer Lightning Jack, is he?"

"'Fraid so."

"Well, he ain't gonna find him."

"I know, but I can't have him traipsing all over the mountain until he stumbles upon my still. The last thing the clan wants is the law in the hollow."

"Got a plan to run him off?"

"The man is downright determined," Jo grumped. "Good Lord willing and the creek don't rise, he'll be gone in three days."

Granny's eyes twinkled. "Unless he's got courtin' on the mind?"

"Oh, no, Granny. I've washed my hands of men." *Even the handsome ones* such as Sullivan.

"Handsome, is he?" Sometimes Granny's "sight" was a bit unnerving.

"Not movie-star handsome. But tall, and he has nice eyes. And he said—" Jo snapped her mouth shut, embarrassed that she carried on about a man she'd met a day ago, even if he was intriguing. Sexy.

"Spit it out, child."

"He inquired about Katie's father and I explained that things didn't work out between us. Then he mentioned he'd grown up without a father, too." It would do Jo no good to develop a soft spot for Sullivan, so she changed the subject. "What are you making?"

"A liniment fer Suzanne."

Suzanne was married to Tom Kavenagh. "Is she worse?"

"Tom said she's havin' trouble gettin' out of bed in the mornin's."

As with many of the clan members, the Kavenaghs had no health insurance and were unable to afford prescription drugs for Suzanne's degenerative arthritis. Most folks in the hollow were self-employed and carried no health plans. Those who worked in the sawmill had insurance but often were unable to miss work to drive to the nearest clinic sixty miles away. Clan members sought Granny's help first before turning elsewhere for medical assistance.

Finding the right balance between old and new was an ongoing struggle for the clan. Government assistance came with strings attached—strings that threatened the clan's customs and traditions. Jobs in the city lured the younger generation away with promises of better health care and employment benefits such as paid vacations and retirement funds.

Granny interrupted Jo's musings. "Whatcha gonna do 'bout yer man."

"The reporter is not my man."

"Then yer enemy." Granny grinned.

Jo sprang from the rocker and paced. "I've got fifty pounds of malting corn ready to sprout that I have to use before it's ruined."

"Have to do yer liquor-makin' at night."

She could sneak off in the wee hours of the morning to work the still but that didn't solve her dilemma during the day. "He needs a babysitter while I'm at the school."

Granny frowned, her wrinkled skin and sagging jowls reminiscent of a bulldog. "Ya askin' me to watch the feller?"

Now that Granny mentioned it... "I'd appreciate you keeping an eye out in case Sullivan wanders."

"I'm goin' twelve ways to Sunday, but I reckon I can drop by yer place."

"Thank you." Jo hugged the smaller woman.

"Take care up at the still."

"I will." Jo left, cutting across the heather fields to pick up the trail. The clan was fortunate to have Granny. The old woman claimed healing was in the genes. One had to be born to it. Jo fretted over who would carry on after Granny was gone. She forced her thoughts from the future, though, the image too bleak and despairing.

SULLIVAN GROANED as he rolled to a sitting position on the hard table in Johanna Macpherson's cookhouse. He rubbed the sleep from his blurry eyes and noticed that his canine guard had abandoned him. Darn dog, probably didn't even wait until daybreak before chasing off into the woods. He checked his watch—8:00 a.m. He never slept this late.

His mouth felt as though he'd chewed cotton all night— probably still dehydrated from his bout with Montezuma's revenge. He dropped his feet to the floor, then made a grab for the table when his muscles cramped and his legs threatened to buckle.

First on his agenda today was a big glass of water, a shower and a clean change of clothes, in that order. At least his abductor had had the sense to grab his duffel before stowing his car wherever the hell she'd hid it. He reached into his pants pocket and removed his cell phone. *Dead.* No surprise, since he hadn't charged the battery in two days. Hopefully Jo hadn't rummaged through his bag and removed the charger. And he prayed his digital camera remained hidden between his socks and underwear. He had no intention of returning to the newspaper without photos of Lightning Jack.

He left the shed, crossed the yard, then paused in front of the porch. A prickly sensation danced down his back. He waited. Listened. Nothing. He climbed the steps and opened the front door, not surprised it was unlocked. One last time he glanced over his shoulder and scanned the woods beyond the cabin. He swore there were eyes on him. Shaking off the eerie feeling, he slipped inside and flipped the bolt.

Jo had left a loaf of homemade bread, still warm from the oven, on the kitchen table. He eyed the loaf, suspecting it was tainted with yet another secret ingredient—perhaps a sleeping potion. He passed on the bread and selected a banana from the fruit bowl. His stomach protested loudly, but settled down when he chased the fruit with a large glass of water. Breakfast out of the way, he plugged the phone charger into the outlet by the kitchen sink, then retreated to the bathroom.

He grimaced at his reflection in the mirror. After retrieving his shaving kit from his duffel, he scraped the stubble from his cheeks, then brushed his teeth twice before selecting a clean change of clothes. He set his outfit on the window ledge next to the tub, wishing Jo had installed a shower nozzle. He'd have to settle for a soak.

Intending to ease the kinks from his aching muscles, he ran the hot tap. Steam filled the tiny room, so he opened the window before easing into the water. He helped himself to a rolled-up hand towel from the wicker basket on the floor, then shoved the cloth behind his neck and closed his eyes, groaning in pleasure. He couldn't survive another night on the table. If Jo refused to allow him to sleep on the couch, he'd fold up in the rocking chair on the front porch.

A few minutes passed and the stiffness faded from his muscles. He grasped the bar of soap and sniffed. Lemon-scented just like Jo's neck. He fantasized about smelling all the different places on Jo's body in search of the citrusy fragrance.

Drag your thoughts out of the gutter, man. Jo was a respectable woman. A mother, for God's sake. As much as the idea of starting something with her intrigued him, he was a guest in her home and he was going to keep his hands to himself even if it killed him.

After working up a lather, he stood and scrubbed his hair first, then his body, until he resembled a giant-sized Mr. Bubble.

As he turned to sit, his gaze passed over the open window and he froze. A face—wrinkled and old, with wandering eyes—gawked at him. Three seconds passed before Sullivan's mind registered the presence of a voyeur. He wasn't certain who screamed first—him, he suspected. He plunged into the water, slipping sideways and ending up with a mouthful of soap bubbles. He gripped the edge of the tub and hauled himself up, sputtering, coughing, burping and wiping at his stinging eyes.

When he caught his breath, he glanced at the window again. A sense of déjà vu swept over him. The barrel of a double-gauge shotgun stared him down. What was it with these hillbillies and guns? Didn't they own any other weapons—nunchucks, swords? *Jo owned a slingshot, remember?*

"May I at least finish my bath before I meet my Maker?" he growled.

The barrel of the gun tilted downward, aiming at his heart, then slowly one gnarled finger uncocked the trigger and the weapon vanished. But the face reappeared. "Get a move on, sonny. Soakin' all day in the tub like a sissy-lickin' city slicker."

Sissy-lickin' city slicker? He doubted the hag could say that three times fast. Sticky with soap residue, he pulled the plug, then hopped out of the tub. When he reached for his clothes, they were gone. Gun or no gun, he'd had enough.

He slung a rust-colored towel around his hips and stormed out of the bathroom, across the cabin and through the front door. The perpetrator sat in a rocking chair, his clothes in her lap and the shotgun resting atop them. "Give 'em back, you old witch!" He cringed when he heard his voice crack.

"Might be old and some folks done accused me of bein' a witch, but I ain't deaf. Quit yer hollerin'."

Feeling vulnerable clad only in a bath towel, Sullivan crossed his arms over his chest. "I want my clothes."

"I've a mind to visit." She eyed him, then nodded to the rocker nearby. "Take a load off."

He swallowed a cussword as he obeyed, then clutched the towel when the flap flew open.

"Name's Granny O'Neil."

"Sullivan Mooreland from Seattle." He clarified. "That's Seattle, Washington."

"I knows 'bout the Space Needle." They rocked in unison, their chairs keeping rhythm with a humming noise off in the distance. He stopped his chair, cocked his head and listened, hoping to identify the sound.

"Sawmill." She pointed northeast.

"Is the mill located in Heather's Hollow?"

Granny nodded. "Them men is busier'n a one-eyed ca scoutin' nine rat holes."

"How big is the hollow?" If he understood the size and scope of the area, he could better plan his search for Lightning Jack.

"Don't rightly know. 'Bout fifty miles north. Twenty west Maybe twenty-five east. Here's where most folks live. Nea Finnegan's Stand. Once ya cross the Periwinkle Creek, yer ou of the holler."

"That's a hell of a lot of mountain the clan owns."

"Years past, the elders done sold off pieces of land to pay the government."

"For taxes, you mean?"

She shrugged.

"Does the government own the mineral rights to the land?" He figured the hollow rested on a fortune in coal.

"Government don't own nothin' in the hollow. But the phone company come out and strung up a few poles in '59."

"What does your husband do?" he asked.

"Nothin'. He's dead."

"I'm sorry."

"Don't make me no never mind no how. 'Expect I'll see him directly."

Directly? As in now? Or as in next year...directly. Wouldn't look good if he was caught trying to revive a dead granny while wearing nothing but a bath towel. "How do yo keep yourself busy?"

"Healin' folks' ails."

"Ah, I was right. You're a witch," he teased.

Her grin showed off a gap between her front teeth. "Got m a few spells up my sleeve. Mostly I make medicines and docto the clan." She squirmed in the chair, the gun slipping lower until the muzzle pointed at Sullivan's crotch. "Experimentin' with a new liniment."

"Liniment for what?" He nudged the barrel in a different direction.

"Rheumatism and arthritis."

"What's in the cream?" He'd need some if he had to spend another night in the cookhouse.

"Heather. Got me a remedy fer bladder infections. Heather tea'll fix ya right and heather honey'll dry up the hay fever."

"Did the hollow get its name from the heather that grows here?" Damn, he wished he had his reporter's notebook handy. Hopefully he'd remember everything the woman said.

"Nah. The old ones done carried heather plants with 'em when they come from Scotland. Cleared a mess of trees off the mountain to plant the fields."

Since the granny appeared talkative—unlike Jo—Sullivan sneaked in the question, "You got any recipes for moonshine?"

"My daddy and granddaddy were whiskey makers." Granny removed a miniature tin from her skirt pocket, pinched off a bit of snuff and stuck the tobacco between her bottom lip and teeth.

"You ever heard of a man called Lightning Jack?"

"Yep."

Sullivan's pulse jumped. "Have you met him?"

"Don't recall."

"Any idea where he lives?"

"Nope."

His pulse returned to normal. "My research claims Lighting Jack lives in Heather's Hollow."

"I reckon he did at one time."

"You think he went into hiding?"

"Might've."

"The bootlegger must be in his eighties or nineties by now. Does he have family making sure he's okay?"

"Just 'cause ya get old don't mean yer useless."

Frustrated, Sullivan shoved a hand through his hair, and his fingers came away sticky. He'd need to have another bath as soon as the old woman wandered off to wherever she'd wandered in from. "It's mighty suspicious that no one has ever met the man or recalls where he lives."

Granny's one-eyed glare dared Sullivan to call her a liar.

"Maybe you can explain why Jo is determined to force me off the mountain."

"She don't want ya here 'cause yer katty-wonkered."

"Katty-wonkered? What the hell does that mean?"

"Crooked."

"Wait a minute. I haven't done anything illegal," he protested.

A mouthful of tobacco juice sailed into the bushes to the side of the porch. "Maybe not yet, but ya sure is nib-nosed."

"What is it with you people? Don't any of you speak plain English?"

"What Granny means is you're nosy."

His heart thumped wildly at the sound of Jo's voice. He swung his head sideways and swallowed hard. She stood at the far end of the porch, looking very *hot* in a pair of faded jeans with a tear in the knee and a cotton T-shirt that molded her breasts to perfection. "Where's the truck?" he snapped, hoping to conceal his reaction to her.

Jo ignored the question. "Do you always entertain in nothing but a bath towel?"

Sullivan pointed to Granny. "She stole my clothes."

"Granny, give the nibby reporter his clothes."

"I was just funnin' with him."

The pile of clothes smacked Sullivan in the face.

"Am I done babysittin'?" Granny asked.

Outraged, he glared. "You hired an old woman to babysit me?"

Jo's gaze dropped to the towel around his hips. "Had I expected you to be this entertaining, I'd have taken the first watch."

"What do you mean, first watch?" He willed a particular part of his anatomy not to react to her feminine perusal.

"Means you're going to meet more of my neighbors over the next few days."

Jo's overly sweet smile clanged like a warning bell inside Sullivan's head.

Chapter Five

Jo struggled to refrain from laughing at Sullivan's gape-jawed expression. What had he expected—that she'd leave him to his own devices while she taught school?

"'Bout time ya showed up," Granny grumbled. "The fool could yakkity-yak the legs off 'n iron pot."

What a sight—an old woman cradling a double-barrel shotgun rocking alongside a half-naked man. "Thanks for your help, Granny." Too bad Jo hadn't thought of stealing Sullivan's clothes this morning. Then she wouldn't have had to impose on the clan healer.

"Are you going to call her off now?" Sullivan nodded to the gun muzzle pointed at his chest.

"For heaven's sake, Granny, put down the gun. If he makes a dash for freedom, he won't get far in a towel." Jo allowed her gaze to wander over Sullivan's naked chest and she conceded the man was sighworthy. He wasn't overly muscular like the clan blacksmith, Tom Kavenagh. The newspaper reporter had a sleek, wiry build. The light golden hair covering his chest narrowed into a thin line that trailed down his stomach and disappeared beneath the… She forced her gaze from his you-know-what and ignored the smirk on his face.

"I'm hungry," Granny announced, eyes twinkling. She

shoved the rifle into Jo's hands. "He's yer problem. I'm fixin' to eat my vittles." The old woman went into the house and shut the front door, leaving Jo and Sullivan to face off.

"Where's Katie?" he asked, scanning the yard behind her.

"With a friend."

The news they were alone must have emboldened Sullivan because he left the rocker, crossed the porch and stood before her. With concentrated effort, she focused on his face. "Granny's not so bad once you get used to her."

"Did you plan to assign guards to me the next three days?" He descended one step.

The scent of lemon bath soap greeted her nose. "Yes."

He raised his arm and grasped the pillar, striking a sexy pose. "What are you afraid of, Jo?"

You. Your sexy body. Her heart thumped an extra beat. She'd never reacted this way to Brian. "You're a stranger in the hollow. For safety reasons, you shouldn't wander without an escort."

One eyebrow lifted at the outer corner, challenging her explanation. He shoved away from the post and descended another step, and another, until his naked chest was inches from her face. "You're afraid I'll run into Lightning Jack, is that it?"

"No." She licked her suddenly dry lips. God help her, she was attracted to this man. Why him? Why another flatlander?

The faint hiss of his indrawn breath alerted her to the notion that he might be just as smittten with her as she was with him. She hoped not. For both their sakes, one of them had to remain sensible.

He rubbed his thumb down her cheek and she jumped inside her skin. "You've scratched yourself." His husky voice feathered over her face. Her eyes stung against the caress. Why did Sullivan have to be such a nice nuisance? She didn't need his kind of complication in her life. Falling in *like*—because that was all she could afford to give up to this man—would make his leaving the hollow more difficult.

Sullivan was nice, sexy and dangerous—a lethal combination. He unnerved her, unbalanced her, yet excited and frustrated her. Being in proximity with him for any length of time would cause tremendous grief and stress and bouts of arousal. The sooner he returned to his own world, the better.

She pressed her hand to her cheek, searching for the cut. He clasped her wrist, guiding her to the wound. Instead of releasing his grip, he moved the pads of his fingers across her palm. Out of the corner of her eye, she noticed the towel twitch.

As if her mouth had a will of its own, she tilted her chin, bringing their lips closer. The heat of his breath bathed her face and she ached to discover the taste of his kiss. Slowly he lowered his head.

Bang!

Sullivan dropped her hand and retreated to the top step, a swath of red spreading across his chest and up his neck. *Amazing.* She'd never seen a man blush like that.

"Company's comin'," Granny announced, her eyes trained on the empty road.

"I don't see anyone," Sullivan argued.

Trusting Granny's instincts, Jo watched the road. Sure enough, a moment later the sputter of a car engine filled the air. Jo was saved from analyzing her and Sullivan's almost kiss by the rusted 1975 two-door blue Gremlin barreling up the dirt drive. *Annie.*

Jo tossed the shogun to Sullivan and rushed to the car, hoping nothing had happened to Katie. Granny followed, flying down the stairs faster than was safe for a woman of advanced age.

"Come quick!" Annie called, scrambling from the driver's seat.

A sigh of relief escaped Jo after she stuck her head into the car and noticed her daughter wave from the back seat. Assured that Katie was fine, she demanded, "What happened?"

"Tommy and Bobby got into a fight."

"At school?" Jo exclaimed. "I left the building less than twenty minutes ago." She cast Sullivan a this-is-your-fault glare. Because she hadn't trusted the flatlander not to run off, she'd risked leaving the older kids alone to check that Granny had arrived at the cabin.

"Wait until their father hears about this." Annie wailed.

In Jo's opinion, her friend had spouted an empty threat. Annie's husband had never been a disciplinarian and now that he worked away from home in the mines, he wasn't around to help Annie keep the boys in line.

"What was they arguin' 'bout?" Granny joined the women.

"Chores." Annie peered around Jo's shoulder. "What are you staring at, pervert?"

Sullivan leaned the shotgun against the house and retreated behind the screen door. *Smart man.* Annie's spitfire temper was well recognized among clan members.

"C'mon, Granny. I threatened to break the boys' legs if they moved off the school steps."

Katie crawled over the front seat and scrambled from the car. "Can I stay here, Mama?" She hugged Jo's leg.

Granny slipped into the passenger side, while Annie got into the driver's seat. "I'm sorry, Jo. I can't take care of Katie today. The boys have got me too agitated."

"Don't worry. I'll meet you at the school in a few minutes."

After the Gremlin drove off, Katie tugged Jo's shirt. "Ms. Annie's mad at Mr. McKee 'cause she said he's never home to catch Tommy and Bobby being naughty."

"As soon as Granny finishes doctoring them, Ms. Annie will calm down." Jo shifted her gaze between the shadow standing behind the screen door and her daughter. Did she dare leave Katie alone with Sullivan? He appeared to be a respectable guy, but for all intents and purposes she knew zip about the man except that he was single and a reporter. And he'd grown up without a father. And he had a sexy body. Shoot, he could be a child molester parading as a newspaper reporter!

Good grief, Jo. A child molester wouldn't have almost kissed you a few minutes ago. Still… "You'll have to go with me, honey."

Katie crossed her arms over her chest and stuck her lower lip out. "Nuh-uh."

"Don't get sassy with me, young lady."

"Mr. Sully's nice. I wanna stay with him, Mama."

Indecision warred inside Jo. Kids had good instincts when it came to trusting adults. If her daughter felt safe around Sullivan… Her gaze moved to the screen door.

"Oh no you don't," Sullivan protested. He stepped onto the porch, clutching the pile of clothes to his chest. "You can't leave her here with me."

His protest put her mind at ease. If he meant Katie harm, he'd be giddy at the prospect of being left alone with her. "Why not?" She propped her fists on her hips. "You caused this ruckus."

"Me?" Indignation echoed in his voice.

"I wouldn't have left my students unattended at school if I hadn't worried about you sneaking off."

"Sneaking off? For crying out loud, Jo, I'm trying to find a way to *stay.*"

"You mean, stick your nose into private business," she accused. In the back of her mind she questioned this man's ability to stir her emotions. She went from amused, to sexually aroused, to frustrated, to angry within seconds. She suspected a day, let alone a lifetime with Sullivan, would put any woman into an early grave.

"Lightning Jack's a public figure. Are you aware he's wanted by the FBI?"

Federal Bureau of Investigation? Good Lord, the FBI was a heck of a lot more serious than the local sheriff's deputy stumbling across her still. One would throw her into the slammer, and the other would slap her hand and issue a warning. Darn it, she should have tried harder to find a legal means to pay for her educational programs. Maybe she'd overlooked a grant or endowment that didn't have strings attached. Jo made a mental promise to herself to put more effort into securing legitimate funding for the school—as soon as she got rid of the reporter. She knelt in front of Katie. "I'll allow you to stay with Mr. Sully provided you follow the same rules as if Granny were here."

Katie nodded solemnly. Jo kissed her cheek, then gave her daughter a gentle push. "Go inside and get a juice box while I speak to Mr. Sully." Jo followed Katie up the porch steps.

After her daughter went into the house, she grabbed the shotgun and delivered her threat in a hushed voice. "If one hair on that child's head is out of place…you'll be off searching for your Maker, not Lightning Jack, understood?"

Sullivan swallowed hard. "I don't know anything about taking care of kids."

"Don't worry, she's potty-trained. Besides, I expect she'll be the one watching over you." Then Jo added, "Beware of the dog. Jelly will attack anyone who tries to harm Katie." She stuck her fingers in her mouth and whistled. The huge dog bounded out of the woods. "Stay with Katie," Jo said to the animal. Understanding the command, the dog trotted across the yard and up the porch steps, where he settled by the door. Satisfied, Jo headed for the woods, where she'd parked the truck a quarter mile up the trail.

"When do you plan to return?" he shouted.

"As soon as the students finish their essays."

"How long will that be?"

"Hopefully before you get yourself into another pickle," she grumbled, then slipped through the underbrush and disappeared.

SULLIVAN STOOD in the front yard, convinced he must be the most hardheaded man alive. If he knew what was good for him, he'd pack his bag and get the hell off the mountain, and search for a different story to write. Too bad he yearned to do what wasn't good for him—track down Lightning Jack and finish the kiss he'd almost started with Jo.

"Hey, Mr. Sully. You wan' a juice box?" Katie offered him a drink.

Squelching lecherous thoughts of the child's mother, Sullivan studied the redheaded leprechaun in jean overalls and a blue-and-white checked shirt. Darn kid was too cute for her own good. "What flavor?"

"Banana Bash."

Gross. "Thanks." He sucked down the drink and tried not to wince at the awful taste. "After I put on my clothes, we're going into town."

"Uh-oh." Crystal-clear blue eyes blinked.

"Uh-ho, what?" He moved past Katie and entered the house. The kid followed. "Mama said I have to stay inside."

At the bathroom, he paused. "Wait here." He changed clothes quickly, ignoring the sticky soap residue on his skin and hair. When he opened the door, he almost mowed down the elf. "What are you doing?"

"Waitin' 'cause you said so."

He questioned his coworkers who complained that their kids never listened to them. *Must be bad parenting on their part.* He retrieved his cell phone from the charger on the kitchen counter and stuffed it into his jean pocket. "Let's go."

"But I'll get into *big* trouble if I don't stay here." Katie dogged his heels.

"Well, we've got a problem then. I have to leave."

"Why?"

Were all kids this inquisitive? "I need to call my boss, and my cell phone doesn't work in the hollow."

"Mama doesn't have to go to town when she talks on her cell phone."

Sullivan stopped in the middle of the yard. "Your mother has a cell phone?" He never would have guessed the wilderness woman was a fan of text messaging.

The leprechaun's chin rose in the air. *Like mother like daughter.* "I know how to use it, too."

"Good for you." He scanned the area. "Where does your mother make her calls?"

"At grandpa's cabin."

The fishing cabin? A shudder rippled through his body at the bad memories. However, if there was a cell tower near there… "Okay. Lead the way."

Short arms crossed over a skinny chest. "Nope. I gotta stay in the house."

"One call." He held up a finger. "Your mother won't even realize we left."

"Not gonna work," Katie warned.

"Why not?"

"'Cause Mama'll find out."

"How?"

She lifted her hands in the air and shrugged. "She always knows when I break a rule."

Think, Sullivan, think. What if he left the child behind and went off on his own? No, he couldn't. He'd promised Jo he'd watch out for her daughter. He eyed the dog at Katie's side. "Jelly will be along to guard us." The guys at the paper would laugh him out of a job if they discovered he'd used a six-year-old and a dog as a guide.

Katie shook her head. The elf was as stubborn as her mother. "If I don't call my boss, I might lose my job." An exaggeration, but desperate people said stupid things.

Brow scrunched, she considered his words. "Can you get another job?"

He sighed heavily, holding back a smile. "No, I'm afraid not."

"Okay, but we have to hurry."

That was easy. "Promise." He walked off at a brisk pace, but stopped when he wasn't sure what direction to go in. "Which way?" he asked when Katie caught up to him.

She shyly slid her hand into his. "Mama holds my hand so she doesn't lose me."

Holding her small hand caused a funny feeling in his chest. If he wasn't careful, his strong fingers might crush her tiny bones.

"C'mon, Jelly!" Katie headed in the direction of the path Jo had taken a short while ago.

After five minutes on the trail Sullivan got a bad feeling. He'd paid particular attention to his surroundings, attempting to identify landmarks for their return hike, but after a while the flowers, trees and weeds blended into one gigantic foliage screen. "Are we walking in circles?"

"Nope." She pointed ahead to the left. "Grandpa's cabin is thatta way."

He'd have to trust the kid. "What were you doing this morning?"

"I was at Ms. Annie's house. She babysits me when I don't go to school with Mama."

"Where does Ms. Annie live?"

"By Granny." Without sucking in a breath, she added, "Tommy and Bobby have a tree house and I get to play in it."

Sullivan suspected the distraught woman who'd called him a pervert had nothing to do with the famous bootlegger, but one of her acquaintances might have knowledge of Lightning

Jack's whereabouts. "Does Ms. Annie do anything other than babysit kids?"

"No, but Mr. McKee works in the big mine."

"Coal mine?"

"Yep." Katie tugged on his hand and pointed at a withered shack several yards ahead, then ran full speed down the trail, where Jelly waited, tail wagging. The little girl coaxed the dog up onto the cabin porch, and they sat together. Sullivan removed his cell phone from his pants pocket and flipped it open. No signal. "Are you sure your mom makes her calls here?"

"Up there." Katie pointed skyward.

"Where?" His gaze followed her finger.

Finger still aimed at the clouds, she strolled toward him. "Don't you see it?"

"Where?"

"The big tree."

He identified an evergreen five stories high, walked over to the tree, stood beneath its massive branches and tried the phone again. Nothing. "Is this a joke, Katie? I'm not getting a signal."

She rolled her eyes. "That's 'cause you gotta climb the tree."

What? No way would Jo scale a tree that tall. Then Sullivan noticed wooden pegs had been pounded into the trunk every few feet until they disappeared beneath the branches. Sweat broke out across his forehead. He'd hated heights since the day he'd attempted to retrieve his personal possessions from an apartment he and his mother had been evicted from. His foot had slipped and he'd tumbled from the second-story balcony. Ended up with a broken ankle and scraped face.

From that day on he'd preferred basement or first-floor apartments, cars that hugged the road and a twentieth-floor cubicle away from the windows.

After assuring his boss that he was on top of a great story, Sullivan proposed to ask his coworker to uncover as much information as possible about Johanna Macpherson. Reporter's instinct assured him Jo had a connection to Lightning Jack. Damned if he could figure out what it was. "Stay here with Jelly. I'm going up."

Katie and the dog returned to the porch. Satisfied the child was safe, he began climbing. "Tell me when I'm high enough," he instructed.

"Okay, Mr. Sully."

After ascending several feet, he hollered, "Am I high enough now?"

"Nope!"

Another two feet. "What about now!"

"No!"

Don't look down. Don't look down. Several more feet.

"Stop, Mr. Sully!"

Air rushed from his lungs, leaving him dizzy. How long had he been holding his breath? He withdrew the cell phone from his pocket, flipped it open with one hand and pressed three.

After several rings… "Baker here."

"Howard. Sullivan Mooreland."

"Where the hell are you, Mooreland?"

"You don't want to know, sir." Sullivan spotted a black spider crawling along the bark inches from his nose. He gripped the handhold tighter. "I assure you that I'm on top of things—" *literally* "—and that I'll have something for you by the end of the week."

"I hope so, Sullivan. If your story is as good as you promised, I'll consider you for the editor position."

"Thank you, sir. Would you transfer me to Ed's desk?"

"Hold on."

Ed came on the line. "I have a favor to ask," Sullivan stated, wasting no time on niceties. "Find out everything you can about a woman named Johanna Macpherson."

"Not that you care, I'm the proud father of another baby girl. Mary and I named her Ruth, after Mary's mother."

"Congratulations, Ed. Did you write that name down—Johanna Macpherson?"

"Johanna who?"

"Mac—" Sullivan ducked when an unidentifiable object torpedoed him from the branches above his head. Panic-stricken, he glanced down. *Shit.* His head spun and his stomach plummeted. And the phone slipped from his sweaty grasp! "No-o-o—" He was cut off in midscream by a large bird with long talons that flew so close, its wings ruffled Sullivan's hair. "Katie! Catch my phone!"

"My, my, my. Did Jeb's hounds tree you, Sullivan?"

Jo? He resisted glancing down, lest he freefall to his death. "Is my phone down there?"

"Yep."

"Where is it?"

"Squashed under my boot. You plan to climb down any time soon?"

"I can't."

"Can't what?"

"Climb down."

"You're kidding."

"Would I be hugging a tree if I was joking?"

Chapter Six

Oh, good grief. What had she done to deserve such a stupid man crashing into her life? Stupid and *sexy*, a voice in her head added. Jo faced her daughter, who'd joined her under the tree. "What were you thinking? You broke a rule and left the house."

"Don't get mad at her. It's my fault," Sullivan protested from the clouds.

"I'm sorry, Mama." Her daughter's lip wobbled.

"Next time you'll be punished." Jo remained firm and resisted the urge to hug the little imp.

"Is anyone going to help me?"

If Katie hadn't been present, Jo would have walked off and left Mr. Reporter to find his own way down from the tree. "Hold on."

Grumbling, she shimmied up the trunk and stopped within a few feet of Sullivan. "I ought to take a switch to your backside for wandering through the woods with Katie."

"I had to phone my boss. Katie was fine."

"No thanks to you. Treed like a cat while my daughter is left to her own devices. What if she'd been attacked by a rabid animal or the bear that's been spotted wandering these woods?"

"The bear story was real?"

"These mountains are as dangerous as they are beautiful, Sullivan. We don't exaggerate for fun."

"You're right. I shouldn't have asked Katie to bring me here. I'm sorry."

Darn him. Why did his apology have to sound sincere? And how did he always manage to twist everything so that she pitied him?

"Move your hand first," she instructed.

"I can't let go," he confessed.

Jo climbed higher, until her face was even with his waist. His nearness messed with her train of thought and she had to force herself to focus, to keep from tumbling to the ground. "Nice and slow. I'll guide your feet."

Sullivan didn't budge. *Great. Now what?* She climbed another rung, her foot sharing the position with his. Her breasts flattened against his back as she attempted to pry his hand loose.

"What are you doing?" His hoarse whisper reminded her of their almost kiss earlier that morning.

"Trying to make you release your grip."

He shifted right, then left, then right again, the friction causing her nipples to tingle.

Clenching her teeth, she hissed in his ear, "If you don't stop wiggling, we'll have a bigger problem than getting you down from this tree."

He swiveled his head and grinned.

Men! "Relax," she insisted, and he allowed her to move his grip to the next peg.

They descended the tree, one foot, one hand at a time. Once both their feet were firmly planted on the ground, she hauled off and socked him in the gut.

Bent over at the waist, he wheezed, "What was that for?"

"That's for putting my daughter in danger."

And for making me want you.

Jo SLOUCHED in a rocking chair on the front porch, watching the sun bed down for the night. After an uncomfortable supper during which Katie carried the conversation, Jo had slipped outside to be alone with her thoughts while her daughter and Sullivan headed for the TV.

The creaking of the screen door, followed by, "Mind if I join you?" ended her peace and quiet.

"Suit yourself."

Sullivan gingerly sank into the other chair, a grunt escaping his mouth.

Guilt gnawed at her, but she shoved the feeling aside. Her life had begun a downward spiral the moment she'd spotted Sullivan on the run from Jeb's dogs. How could this man's mission upend her life? One moment she was going about her business, teaching, making moonshine, raising her daughter. The next she was poisoning a reporter, physically accosting him, then threatening to lash him with a switch. "About slugging you in the gut…"

He waved off her attempt to apologize.

She pressed on. "I'm sorry I lost my temper and stepped on your phone."

"No more than I deserved for coaxing Katie into disobeying you." He chuckled. "She put up a hell of a fight until I told her I might lose my job if I didn't call my boss. Your daughter has a compassionate heart."

Chest swelling with love for her child, Jo agreed, "Katie's a good girl."

"Mind if I ask what happened between you and her father?" Sullivan intended to learn as much about Jo as possible. This afternoon when she'd rescued him from the tree he'd felt more than a sexual response to her touch. She'd made him feel safe. Made him yearn to trust her. He couldn't remember ever depending on anyone, especially a woman. The stretch of silence confirmed that Jo didn't plan to answer his question. "Never mind. It's none of my—"

"If you tell me about the women in your life, I'll talk about Katie's father."

"Fair enough." Hell, there wasn't much to tell. "I'm not involved with anyone at the moment. I've had two long-term relationships that each lasted about one month."

"You consider a month long-term?"

He shrugged. "That's about the length of time it takes for a woman to figure out I have no desire to marry." But neither of the women had been anything like Johanna Macpherson. Had they been, he would have given a long-term commitment serious contemplation.

"You don't want to get married…ever?"

"I was determined to put my career first. Long hours and weekend deadlines don't mix well with having a family." He switched his attention from Jo's face to the shadows beyond the porch. "Now…I don't know."

"Why the change of heart?"

Unable to resist the pull of her hushed voice, he studied her and decided he wouldn't mind waking each morning to her face on the pillow next to his. Her long red hair tangling with his beard stubble. Her breath puffing against his neck. Legs entwined. Hands seeking private places. "I'm sorry, I forgot what I was about to say."

Her white teeth flashed in the darkness, then she wiggled around and set her chair rocking. "I was student teaching at a high school in Lexington when I met Brian. He coached the boys' junior varsity-basketball team."

An athlete. *Figures.* Jealousy tugged at Sullivan's gut. As a kid, he'd yearned to play sports. Lack of money and his mother's overindulgence in alcohol had nixed those dreams.

"Brian was tall and handsome, and he drove an expensive car," she continued. "He wined and dined me at five-star restaurants."

Ah. That explained her reaction to his Corvette.

"When I asked how he paid for such a lifestyle on a teacher's salary, he confessed that his family dabbled in horses."

"Dabbled in horses?" Sullivan had trouble picturing a person dabbling in a horse.

"They raised and trained Kentucky Derby Thoroughbreds."

Handsome and wealthy—two things Sullivan wasn't.

"His folks owned a plantation on the outskirts of Lexington. For a girl who'd grown up among plow horses, I was wowed by the expensive horseflesh, the elaborate barns, the jockeys and, of course, the big mansion with white pillars."

After living in seedy apartments and broken-down cars, Sullivan would have reacted the same way.

"His parents were friendly until they learned I hailed from Heather's Hollow. Their shocked expressions said they didn't believe an Appalachian mountain girl was good enough for their son. Stupidly I'd convinced myself that they'd change."

At the wistful note in Jo's voice, Sullivan grasped her hand. He threaded his fingers through hers and squeezed. "Let me guess. They never came around."

Jo nodded. "But his parents had nothing to do with the reason Brian broke up with me."

When Jo attempted to remove her hand from his hold, he tightened his fingers around hers. No matter how at odds they were over his goal to locate Lightning Jack, he cared about her. Cared that Brian, the jerk, had hurt her.

"Brian pressured me for sex, but I wished to wait until we were officially engaged. He promised he'd propose after I graduated in the spring. I bought into his lie." Jo vaulted from the rocking chair. She stood with her back to Sullivan. "Eventually he wore me down and I gave in. I expected a proposal to follow. One week turned into two. Then three. Then I discovered I was expecting Katie. When I told Brian..."

"Don't, Jo." Sullivan left his chair. The urge to ease her pain felt foreign to him. "The guy's an ass." He stroked the fiery curls brushing her shoulders, the silky strands clinging to his fingertips.

"I'm not turn-your-head pretty." She kept her face hidden in the shadows but leaned into his touch—as if yearning for reassurance that she was desirable. That any man would want her. That *he* wanted her.

"I believed Brian loved me. Instead he exploited me. I was nothing more than a bet—a wager with his high-society buddies that he could coax the redneck girl into his bed."

Damn, he hungered to flatten Brian's nose for hurting Jo. "What did he say when he found out he'd gotten you pregnant?"

"He denied he was the father. Got his friends to lie and say they'd slept with me, too."

The guy was a schmuck. "What about a paternity test? You have a right to child support."

"Brian warned me not to mess with him or his family. That they had connections in high places and my petition would end up in some judge's garbage can."

"I'm sorry, Jo." He slid his hand beneath her hair and stroked her neck, rubbing his thumb against the skin below her ear.

"Doesn't matter. Everything worked out for the best. My daughter and I have each other. We wouldn't have been happy living in Brian's world."

"Come here." Sullivan coaxed her into his arms, ignoring her stiff posture. "You've done a great job raising Katie on your own."

"Not on my own," she protested, her voice muffled by the

front of his shirt. "I don't know what I would have done if Grandpa... Katie was a colicky baby and he walked the floors with her every night for months. And Granny and Annie were a big help, too." She placed her hands against his chest and forced several inches of space between them. "That's what's special about living in the hollow, Sullivan. We're one big family." Her blue eyes begged him to understand something he'd never experienced in his life.

Envy stabbed him. He'd always wished for a mother who didn't drink. For a father who would claim him. For sisters and brothers to play and argue with. Maybe that was what drew him to Jo and Katie. They were surrounded by people who loved them and he'd been alone all his life. He lowered his head, then paused inches from her mouth and waited. *Don't refuse me, Jo. I'm dying to taste you.*

Her sigh floated into his mouth as she settled her lips against his.

Mmm. Vanilla—the ice cream they'd eaten for dessert.

Good Lord, Sullivan. Where in the world did you learn to use your tongue that way?

Open wider. I want more.

My head is spinning.

Why the hell are my legs shaking?

Jo went up on tiptoe, shoved her breasts against his chest and coiled her arms around his neck. *Ah...perfect.*

Let me touch you. He moved his hands up her back and around her rib cage, nudging the sweet curves of her breasts. Shifting sideways, she brought the mounds in full contact with his palms.

Gently, he rubbed his hands across the hardening nipples. Squeezed, massaged until he thought he'd die if he didn't taste the treasure he held.

"Whatcha doin' kissin' Mr. Sully, Mama?"

Katie! Jo stumbled back so suddenly that if not for his quick reflexes, she'd have fallen off the porch and landed on her rump in the dogwood bushes.

"We weren't kissing, young lady." Sullivan faced Katie. "Your mother had something in her eye and I was helping her…find it."

Oh, brother. "Time for bed, honey." Jo moved past Sullivan, ignoring the tingle in her arm where their skin made contact. After ushering her daughter into the house, she said, "Go brush your teeth." As soon as the bathroom door shut, Jo whirled and stared at Sullivan through the screen door. "That shouldn't have happened."

"But it did."

"No more kisses." She glanced over her shoulder to make sure Katie remained out of hearing range.

"Okay," he agreed.

That's it? No protest? No contending their kiss was out of this world? That he couldn't keep his hands off her? *What a turd!* Angry at herself for expecting more and for allowing herself to become caught up in the moment, she huffed, "To-morrow you're leaving the hollow."

"You promised three days. How was I supposed to inter-view the locals for my story when Granny attached herself to me like a bloodsucking leech and then you forced me to baby-sit your daughter?"

His hangdog expression tugged Jo's guilt strings, but she ig-nored the tweak. "There is no story, Sullivan. You've wasted your time and mine." She braced herself for an explosion, but thankfully he spun on his heel and stormed off the porch. She hated that she'd instigated the argument, but if she hadn't, she would have ended up in Sullivan's bed tonight—or he in hers. Not going to happen. She had moonshine to make.

"Ready, Mama." Katie stood in the bathroom doorway, a dab of toothpaste clinging to her chin.

"Let's go chase the bedbugs away." Jo held out her hand and

together they climbed the stairs to the loft. She'd read Katie two books, then tucked the covers around the child's shoulders.

"I like Mr. Sully, Mama."

Jo's fingers paused above the light switch.

"'Cause he makes me laugh."

Oh, honey. Don't lose your heart to the reporter. Her daughter longed for a father. Longed for a traditional family, with two loving parents and siblings. For a while Annie's husband had included Katie in fishing trips with the boys but now that he worked in the Blue Mine, he had so little time with his family that Jo had kept Katie away.

"Does Mr. Sully make you laugh, Mama?"

Make me laugh? Hardly. The exasperating man aggravated her, aroused her… That thought brought a smile to her face.

Katie's giggle startled Jo out of her reverie. Her daughter rolled to her side and snuggled into the pillow. "'Night, Mama."

"Sweet dreams, baby." Jo flipped the light switch and left.

Deciding to check on Sullivan, she poked her head out the front door, but he was nowhere in sight. She wasn't certain if she was disappointed or relieved that he'd gone to bed. After locking the doors, she stretched out on the couch and grabbed the TV remote. An hour later she awoke with a start to a strange animal call.

The boys.

Jo sprang from the couch, turned off the TV, then fetched a flashlight from the kitchen drawer. She stepped onto the porch and spotted Jelly sleeping next to the rocking chair. "Guard Katie, Jelly," she whispered. Cutting across the yard, she walked toward the area where she'd instructed Annie's boys to wait.

After breaking the no-fighting rule at school, she'd given Tommy and Bobby a choice—a week of summer classes or guard duty tonight. They'd chosen guard duty.

"Over here," a voice greeted her, when she wiggled through the dense brush at the back of the property. Wearing camouflage clothing, their faces smeared with black shoe polish, the brothers squatted behind an overgrown honeysuckle bush, the whites of their eyes visible in the dark.

"I appreciate you both taking this mission seriously." Jo swallowed a laugh. Dressed as they were, she couldn't tell them apart.

"He ain't goin' nowhere, Ms. Macpherson," one of them boasted as he lifted a hunting rifle off the ground.

Oh, dear. "Under no circumstance will you shoot or threaten to shoot anyone tonight, understood?"

"Yeah, we figured. Mom hid our bullets."

Thankful for Annie's foresight, Jo motioned to the dark lumps on the ground. "What are those?"

"Sleepin' bags in case we get tired. We're takin' shifts."

"I'd rather you both remain awake. Mr. Mooreland is not to leave the yard."

"He won't," they chimed in unison, flashing white-toothed grins.

"What makes you certain he won't get away?" she asked.

"'Cause we booby-trapped the shed."

"Booby-trapped?" She shoved aside a clump of foliage and squinted at the cookhouse. Nothing appeared amiss.

"We rigged the door with fishin' line. If he escapes, he'll get tangled in a spiderweb."

"And Tommy stuck a bell up there." Bobby pointed to the small cherry tree behind the shed. "If the fishin' line's cut, the bell's gonna fall and clang so we'll know he's on the loose."

Good Lord, she wouldn't want to be in Sullivan's shoes if he attempted to flee tonight. "You guys thought of everything."

"Don't worry, Ms. Macpherson. We can handle him."

"Carry on, soldiers." Jo waved to the boys, then veered north along the trail. After a half mile she spotted the two bushes that had been hacked to the ground at the entrance to a path, which meandered in an easterly direction. The still remained hidden a half mile farther into the woods on land that had belonged to her grandfather's family for generations. Save for the clan elders, none of the locals knew the location of her illegal venture.

Others in the clan had stills on their land and made whiskey for personal consumption, not resale. The local law ignored those folks. Jo, on the other hand, sold her whiskey on the black market and paid not one cent of tax on her profit. Therefore, if the law discovered the location of her still, she was in *big* trouble.

That she was going against the strictly held social mores of the clan didn't sit right with her. In the beginning, she admitted that she'd gotten caught up in the nostalgia of bootlegging. Her clan had a deep tradition of being accountable to no one—not even the law. But this wasn't the 1800s and the old-timers, like her grandfather, who'd been raised believing bootlegging was an acceptable activity, were fast disappearing.

Jo shuddered to think how parents in the hollow would react if they discovered their children's teacher taught by day and broke the law by night. Maybe Sullivan's presence in the hollow was a warning that Jo's bootlegging days were numbered.

With a flip of her fingers, she switched on the flashlight as she traipsed through the underbrush. She wasn't afraid in the dark. Most nights the wildlife left her alone. If a raccoon or possum paid her a visit, she'd chase if off with a few pokes from the three-pronged stick she used to stir the mash.

Fifteen minutes later, the sound of rushing water from Periwinkle Creek greeted her ears. Her grandfather had constructed the still near the mountain stream so that he had plenty of cold water to fill the cooler barrel. She trudged on, feeling more exhausted than usual. Normally she had no problem staying up late, then teaching the next day. Tonight she suspected the cause of her fatigue was Sullivan.

One moment they were arguing; the next she flat out wanted to kiss him. One minute she was spilling her guts about Brian; the next she wanted to pester Sullivan with questions about his own love life. All this chaos inside her was the result of her not dating. She'd been by herself too long, with only Katie, her students, Granny, Annie and a few other clan members for company.

She yearned for the kind of intimate conversation found with that someone special. She wished to lie in bed at night and share her dreams and troubles with a life partner, instead of keeping everything bottled up inside her. She suspected Sullivan would make a compassionate bedfellow—and wouldn't interrupt or nod off in the middle of her spiel.

When she arrived at Ol' Timey, the name her grandfather had affectionately called the still, she lit the lanterns and went about her business. Constructed from copper sheets that had been molded by beating them against a tree stump with a wooden mallet, the equipment was used for fermenting and heating mash; the ground cornmeal kneaded into a stiff dough that sat and cured until it became sour—hence sour mash.

Next Jo boiled the sour mash, using a three-pronged stick with a wire mesh to stir the glob into the consistency of gravy. After a half hour of mixing, she let the mash boil on its own until the concoction foamed. Once the foam dissipated, the liquid traveled through a system of pipes into a second barrel— the condenser. The third barrel—the cooler—contained water from the stream and had a pipe attached to the unit from which the liquor would drip. The final product would be over a hundred proof. She'd add additional water to make the whiskey drinkable. Her grandfather had taught her to mix the liquor with water in a vial and then shake it. If a bead went around the top of the vial and stayed for five or ten minutes, the liquor was eighty proof and ready to sell.

After shoving more wood into the natural-stone furnace chinked with red clay, she tried not to reflect on her front-porch smooch with Sullivan. Darn it, why did he have to be a good kisser and why did his embrace make her feel safe? The reporter was here to uncover the secret of Lightning Jack, not to play hanky-panky with her. If Sullivan found out the truth and exposed her means of funding the school, she'd land in jail and her daughter would be left without any parent.

The idea that he made her feel secure was plumb dumb. Hadn't she learned her lesson with Brian? Never again would she trust a flatlander with her heart.

An image of Sullivan clinging to the evergreen tree on her grandfather's property surfaced in her mind and she smiled. He was the first man in forever who riled her. Stirred her blood. Made her *yearn*—for something Jo was afraid to admit she desperately wanted.

Love.

"STOP OR YER a dead man, mister."

Sullivan halted in his tracks and peered into the darkness. A weapon poked through the bushes in front of him—the third time in less than two days he found himself starring down the barrel of a shotgun.

"Stupid. You didn't tie the thread tight enough."

"Shut up, Tommy. The bell you stuck up in the tree didn't ring, neither."

"You shut up. If—"

"Excuse me," Sullivan interrupted. "Are you the Tommy and Bobby who were fighting at school?"

"How'd you know our names?" one of the voices asked. An "Ouch!" followed the question.

"You said my name, dumb shi—"

"C'mon out of there," Sullivan demanded, relieved the enemy sounded harmless.

Both boys stepped into view. "Hey, mister, how'd you escape?"

Their faces were painted black and both boys were dressed like commandos, so Sullivan wasn't sure which kid had asked the question. "When I discovered the door was blocked, I crawled out the window."

"Told you we shoulda run the fishin' line around the shed," one of them grumbled.

"Why are you guys camping out on Ms. Macpherson's property?"

"We aren't camping out. We're doing a…a recon…thing."

"Reconnaissance?" Sullivan swallowed a laugh.

"Yeah, that."

"And I'm the mission?"

"Ms. Macpherson said we gotta keep you from following her tonight."

Jo had snuck off? Maybe she intended to meet with Lightning Jack and warn the bootlegger that Sullivan was searching for him. "Following her where?"

"Don't know," the boys answered in unison.

"What are you getting paid to play marines? I'll double Ms. Macpherson's payment if you turn your backs while I escape."

"Aw, shucks, mister. We're not getting paid. Mom would skin us alive if she found out we disobeyed the teacher."

"Who's going to tell? I promise to return before Ms. Macpherson."

The brothers glanced at each other. "How much you gonna pay?" one asked.

"Ten bucks," Sullivan proposed.

"Ten each."

"You drive a hard bargain." Sullivan dug his wallet from his pants pocket and handed over a twenty-dollar bill. "Be right back." He entered the cookhouse through the window, removed his digital camera from the duffel and exited back out the window. "Leave the fishing line up," he instructed the boys. "That way Ms. Macpherson won't suspect I escaped. Now, which direction did she head?"

"Thatta way." Both marines pointed up the trail.

Sullivan checked his watch. Almost 1:00 a.m. "You guys carrying an extra flashlight?"

One of the twins handed him a small pocket light—the kind ophthalmologists flash in your eye. "Thanks," he muttered. "No running off. Katie's asleep in the house. If there's an emergency, ring the bell in the tree."

"Don't worry, mister, we won't abandon our post." Both soldiers saluted.

Sullivan mimicked the gesture, then jogged into the night. After fifteen minutes of flashing the penlight into the woods, he spotted a gap in the foliage—a hole that suspiciously marked the entrance to a narrower path leading deeper into the forest. He cocked his head and listened—nothing but an occasional hoot from a night owl and the rustling of tree branches. He inhaled deeply and thought he detected a faint hint of smoke. A wood-burning stove in a cabin or an illegal still? The possibility of discovering the infamous bootlegger at work was enough to persuade him to take the path.

Keeping his eyes and the penlight trained on the ground, he walked a half mile before catching the sound of gurgling water. He slowed his pace but continued. Up ahead, light glowed from between the branches of a thick barrier of low-growing shrubs. He snapped off the penlight and snuck closer, peering through a gap in the thicket of bushes. *Bingo.*

The small clearing was empty, but someone had been busy making moonshine. He recognized the metal still and the stone furnace from historical pictures he'd run across on the Internet. Lanterns had been lit and placed on old tree stumps. Sullivan used the light to his advantage, snapped a couple of pictures with his camera before making himself comfortable. With any luck, tonight he'd meet Lightning Jack.

He didn't have long to wait. Crunching footsteps alerted him to the presence of the bootlegger, who was dressed in black and wore a dark floppy hat, that concealed the person's face. Sullivan knew immediately it wasn't Lightning Jack—it was Johanna Macpherson! Had the bootlegger hired her to work his still until Sullivan left the hollow? He got pictures of Jo stirring the contents in one of the barrels.

After a while Sullivan's knees hurt from squatting and he shifted, the movement twisting his ankle. He landed hard on his hip, making a racket in the bushes.

"Sullivan Mooreland, is that you hiding in there?"

Damn.

"Show your ornery backside before I burn it in the furnace over yonder."

The threat of having his ass set on fire was enough to coax him from the bushes.

"How long have you been spying on me?" she demanded.

"Long enough to know you're breaking the law. Is this Lightning Jack's still? You work for him, don't you?"

"Of course not."

The denial was a tad too vehement to be credible. "Then what are you doing—making soap?"

Chapter Seven

"Do you work for Lightning Jack?" Sullivan repeated the question as he crept closer.

"Of course not," Jo protested. "This is *my* still."

"A schoolteacher tossing together a batch of moonshine— yeah, right."

Changing the subject, she asked, "Is Katie alone at the house?"

"Jelly's on the porch and the boys agreed to keep an eye on the place." He grinned. "Nice try, by the way."

"How did you slip past them?"

"Didn't. Had to pay a toll—twenty bucks."

"Traitors," she mumbled.

Nodding to the equipment behind her, he persisted, "Show me how all this works."

"No. Go back to the cabin. I'll be along shortly."

"Thanks, but I'll wait for you to finish."

A swearword escaped from under her breath. "That was un-ladylike," he teased. When she didn't rise to the bait, he asked, "What's a pint of that stuff go for?"

"I couldn't say, Sullivan. I'm making this for others in the clan." The lie rolled easily off her tongue. *Drat.* What had she been thinking, recruiting two twelve-year-olds to guard the reporter? She should have made Granny to stay at the cabin.

Granny would have sat on the porch all night with her shotgun aimed at the cookhouse.

"If you need help, holler." He collapsed on the ground and leaned against a tree trunk.

Jo wished she could join him. Lord, she was pooped. With a weary sigh she went about her tasks. Three hours later the sunrise flirted with the eastern sky.

Fifteen minutes after he'd snuggled up to the tree, Sullivan had conked out. She'd considered extinguishing the lanterns and leaving him in the dark, but the sound of him sawing logs had comforted her while she worked. Used to being by herself when she brewed the whiskey, Jo hadn't realized how lonely the job was until Sullivan had remained in camp. What he lacked in conversation, he made up for in cuteness—drooling like a baby.

She poked his shoulder and he jerked to attention. "You okay?"

His concern tugged her heart. "I'm fine. Time to go home."

"Do I get a sample?" He rubbed the sleep from his eyes and stumbled to a standing position, then stretched.

"It's not finished." She forced her attention away from his chest and scooted through a break in the underbrush.

Wobbly on his feet, he tripped and Jo steadied him. He flashed a sappy grin. "I can't even have a tiny sip of the stuff?"

"Not unless you want to burn your mouth. It's still one hundred proof." They walked in silence, side by side, each lost in thought. When they left the trail and entered the clearing at the back of her property, she muttered, "Figures." Both Tommy and Bobby snoozed in their sleeping bags. Jelly lay on the cabin porch, guarding the front door. Despite her exhaustion, she grinned at the fishing line across the cookhouse door. "How'd you escape?"

"Squeezed through the window." He lifted his shirt and pointed to a scratch marring his side. "Battle wound."

The sight of Sullivan's bare skin caused her mouth to go dry. Unable to resist, she pressed her fingertips against the reddened flesh. His stomach muscles flinched at her touch and she jerked her hand away. "That should be cleaned to prevent infection."

"Yes, ma'am." His smile, the one she was ridiculously attracted to—cocky, a little flirty but always challenging—faded to serious.

"What?" For a man who by all accounts should be good with words, he resorted to silent stares too often. Why didn't he speak his mind?

"You're a very pretty woman, Johanna Macpherson."

Her mouth dropped open. She'd received few compliments over the years regarding her appearance. After the way Brian had betrayed her, the nice words he'd once uttered meant nothing. Sullivan tapped a finger under her chin. Embarrassed, she closed her mouth.

"Pack your things," she grumped, annoyed that the patch of skin beneath her chin continued to tingle from his touch. "After breakfast I'll drive you into town to pick up your car." She'd aimed to walk off and leave *him* with *his* jaw sagging, but he clutched her elbow before she'd taken two steps.

"Are you hard of hearing?" He released her arm. "I'm not leaving until I meet Lightning Jack."

Jo massaged her brow, hoping to ease the throb that had been present the instant he'd crashed her brewing party. In no shape to fight the stubborn reporter, she argued, "You're wasting your time."

"Until I have proof the bootlegger doesn't exist, I intend to stick around and be a pain in *your* butt."

"Why me?"

"Because you're hiding something." He ignored her gasp. "Because I believe you know the bootlegger's whereabouts. Because I believe you were working his still. Because—"

"Enough!" Darn! Sullivan refused to go down easy. She gazed at the heavens, imaging her Scotch-Irish ancestors toasting the flatlander's determination and resolve. "Sullivan, I have a daughter to care for, end-of-year exams to grade and, as you witnessed, a *hobby* that requires my attention. I don't have the time or the patience to babysit you."

"You're forcing my hand, Jo." His brown eyes flashed and Jo wondered if the orbs turned the same shade of stormy when he made love to a woman. She retreated—as if the additional foot of space would prevent her from drowning in all that chocolate-colored angst.

"Evidence." He shoved his fingers into the front pocket of his jeans and withdrew an electronic gizmo.

"What evidence?" She peered at the object clenched in his fist.

"This is a digital camera. I've got pictures of the still. And you."

Dear Lord. Pictures? "Pictures don't prove anything," she bluffed.

"They prove you're breaking the law."

"You intend to send me to jail, when I have a daughter who depends on me?"

His shocked expression eased some of the fear building in her gut. He did care about her and Katie—there was that, at least. "The cops wouldn't send you to jail."

Maybe the local sheriff's deputy wouldn't, but there was no telling what a state trooper or other government officials might do. Intending to take his mind off the pictorial evidence, she said, "Refresh my memory. Why are you writing a story about Lightning Jack?"

"I plan to enter the feature story in a national contest. A win will guarantee I receive a promotion to editor." He shuffled several steps away, then faced her, hands fisted at his sides.

From his defensive stance, Jo suspected there was more involved than a simple promotion. "I'm listening."

"I've sacrificed a personal life. Never married. Never had kids. I've worked my way up from the bottom." He poked himself in the chest with his finger. "I've earned the title of editor."

"Aside from *earning* the position, why is the job so important to you?"

"Because it proves I'm the best. I'm invaluable to the newspaper. I'll be the envy of every reporter across the country."

"And it's important that people be jealous of you?" He broke eye contact with her and she suspected her candidness had touched a nerve.

She yearned to clobber the person in Sullivan's past who'd taught him that his self-worth hinged on what others thought of him. "Compromising Katie's security and well-being for your own success hardly seems the action of a person to be envied." As soon as she'd spouted the words, she wanted to yank them back. She was a hypocrite—accusing Sullivan of something she was guilty of. Wasn't she risking Katie's future each time she slunk off to brew moonshine? Each time she made the drive through the mountain to deliver the goods to a buyer?

"You make me sound like a jerk," he accused.

More angry with herself than Sullivan, Jo lashed out. "You barged uninvited into the hollow, demanding information on one of our clan members in order to exploit him and the rest of the clan for your own benefit." In truth, Sullivan was no different from most flatlanders, which made her feelings for him confusing. "You're the same as all the others who don't live in the hollow—you view our clan as substandard. We don't count and therefore you have the right to use us to your advantage."

Her tirade left him speechless, allowing her to suck in a deep breath and continue uninterrupted. "By focusing on Lightning Jack, you're concentrating on one aspect of our clan—an illegal one. Rather than presenting the public an accurate picture of the clan, you'll portray us as a bunch of clueless, law-breaking hillbillies."

"No, I intend to be as objective—"

"How can you be objective when you don't understand our ways? You don't live with us. You aren't one of us."

"Then help me get to know the clan, Jo," he begged. "Aside from Granny and a glare from your friend Annie, my only information source is you. And half the time I suspect you're not telling the truth."

How could she dispute that charge? She had to lie to protect the clan. *Be honest, Jo. You're lying to protect yourself.* Swallowing the lump of guilt lodged in her throat, she argued, "I'm working hard to teach the younger generation to be proud of who they are and where they come from. Sensationalizing Lightning Jack won't help my cause." *If what you say is true, then why haven't you worked harder to acquire funding for the school through legal means?*

Dear God. She'd become the very thing she was trying to overcome.

"Ah, that's where you're wrong, Jo. The added publicity might help you secure federal monies for improvements in the hollow, like a medical clinic. The clan wouldn't have to rely on Granny's herbal remedies."

"If we wanted the government's assistance, we'd ask for it."

"I don't understand."

Finally—he'd admitted he didn't understand. "If the clan accepts government aid, it has to abide by federal guidelines, rules and regulations. We'd lose our autonomy and our culture."

"Isn't that attitude a little pessimistic?"

Tired of arguing, she announced, "Katie will be up in an hour. I'm going to soak in the tub." She'd use the quiet time to rethink her strategy.

Granny claimed life was simpler when one plowed around the stumps—and Sullivan was one big stump.

"MAY I BORROW the truck keys?" Sullivan stood in the shadows watching Jo grade essays for several minutes.

They'd struck a truce of sorts the past three days. He hadn't left the hollow and she hadn't left him—out of her sight. He'd been stuck at the cabin with only a six-year-old for a playmate while Jo had all but ignored him as she completed end-of-the-school-year paperwork. This morning he'd decided he'd go nuts if he didn't find something to occupy his time while he and Jo were at an impasse.

"Why?" She flashed her usual narrow-eyed glance at him before returning her attention to the folder in her lap.

"I plan to pick up a few items in town." He was purposefully vague, hoping she wouldn't ask questions. He wanted to surprise Katie. Jo reached into her pocket, then tossed him the keys. "Feel free to fill the tank."

That was easy. He'd expected an argument. "Aren't you afraid I'll take off with the truck and drive somewhere I shouldn't?"

"You discovered my still. There isn't anything else for you to find."

With a nod, he crossed the yard.

Once he reached Finnegan's Stand, he gassed up, then parked outside the hardware store. When he entered, a bell clanged and immediately a young man, not more than sixteen, appeared.

"Help you?" he inquired.

"I intend to build a tree house for a little girl." Sullivan stood before the checkout counter.

"Okay." The teen gaped.

"Here's the problem. I don't know the first thing about building one or what supplies I'll need."

"How far up the tree's it gonna be?"

Was the teen deaf, dumb or both? "I don't have a clue. I've never built a tree house."

"You got a tree picked out?"

There were hundreds of trees on Jo's property. He was positive he could find a decent-sized one. "Not yet."

"The kid's how old?"

"What does age have to do with anything?" The teen probably believed Sullivan was building the tree house for himself—which maybe he was. Sort of.

"If the kid is little, you don't wanna build it too high off the ground, in case they fall."

Shoot. Sullivan hadn't considered a tree house dangerous, but…

"Or you can put up a rail."

Good advice. "Do you sell plans for building tree houses or play forts?"

That question earned a *duh* glare from the teen. After a few seconds of searching, the boy located a blank sheet of notebook paper and sketched the various stages of construction. "I'm impressed," Sullivan complimented him.

"This is the same one I built when I was ten."

If a ten-year-old could build a tree house, then a thirty-eight-year-old should have no problem. By the time he'd purchased the supplies and arrived at the cabin, it was half past noon. Jo, Katie and the dog were nowhere to be found. Assuming they'd left to visit a neighbor, he decided to begin his project and see how far along he could get before they returned.

After fifteen minutes of searching, he decided on a large maple in the backyard—lower branches were at least twelve inches around and there was no visible damage to the trunk. When he faced the cabin, he noticed the tree stood in view of the kitchen window. Perfect. Jo would be able to keep an eye on Katie while she cooked or puttered in the kitchen.

He made several trips back and forth to the truck, unloading the lumber. He considered waiting for Jo, then nixed the idea. If she was unhappy about the tree house, then maybe she'd rethink her willingness to arrange an interview with Lightning Jack. The sooner he got his story, the sooner he'd get out of her hair—and that was what they both wanted, wasn't it?

An image of him waving goodbye to the Macpherson females passed through his mind. Once he got his story and his promotion—then what? Resume the life he'd had? For the first time, Sullivan realized that his job was all he had. There was nothing wrong with working twelve-hour shifts. Weekends. Holidays.

What nagged him most was the idea of returning to an empty apartment at the end of each day. Worst of all, not knowing what Jo and Katie were up to. How had those two worked their way under his skin in such a short while? Shoving the unsettling thoughts aside, he pulled the tree-house sketch from his pocket and went to work.

Sullivan followed the instructions to a tee, making minor adjustments—okay major adjustments, because his only tools were a saw and a hammer. By the time the sun began dropping in the sky, he was dead tired and hungry and if that wasn't enough to discourage him, the tree house didn't resemble any he'd ever seen.

"What in the world."

Jo's voice startled him. He spun, then grimaced at her incredulous expression. Before he assured her that he'd clean up the mess he'd made, Katie squealed and ran full speed toward him. He dropped the hammer seconds before she barreled into his legs and squeezed one thigh until the limb went numb. "You built me a tree house, Mr. Sully!"

"Sort of." Afraid to make eye contact with Jo, he focused on the cherub's face. "It's not fancy."

"It's the best, Mr. Sully." She wandered closer to the maple, craned her neck and gawked, eyes round. By her reaction, one would have thought she'd been given a pony instead of boards nailed haphazardly between tree limbs. "How do I get up there?"

"I have to a nail the steps against the trunk, and it needs a roof." He joined Katie beneath the tree. "And then I'll add a rail, so you won't fall."

Slipping her small hand into his, she declared, "I can help build the rail."

Sullivan's chest throbbed and he rubbed at the annoying twinge. Was he catching a cold? "You'll have to check with your mom, Katie." Embarrassed, he faced Jo and confessed, "I could use your help, too."

As Jo approached, he braced himself for her anger, but instead was caught off guard by the tears welling in her eyes. He'd made her cry? "I'm sorry, Jo. I should have asked first, but Katie mentioned Tommy and Bobby had a tree house and then I remembered I'd always wanted a play fort when I was a kid and, well, one thing led to another and…" He shoved a hand through his hair. "I've made a mess of things, haven't I?"

Rather than giving him a lecture, Jo clasped his face between her hands and whispered, "That's the nicest thing anyone has ever done for my daughter. Thank you, Sullivan." She kissed his cheek. "I'd be happy to help you finish the tree house." Then she held her hand out to Katie and announced, "I bet Mr. Sully is hungry from working so hard. Let's go fix him supper."

Hand in hand the two females walked off—this time leaving Sullivan with his mouth hanging open.

ON WEDNESDAY MORNING, Sullivan found himself standing at the end of the dirt road where Jo had dropped him off. As she drove away, Katie waved out the window. Between breakfast and grabbing a quick bath Jo had informed him that he'd be visiting the clan blacksmith today. When he's asked why she'd changed her mind about letting him interview clan members, she'd claimed to prove once and for all that Lightening Jack wasn't around.

The tree-house plan had succeeded. He, Katie and Jo had worked together the past three days to finish the slightly off-kilter playhouse. Jo had sewn curtains for the one window they'd installed and she'd placed an old rug to cover the floor. A doll cradle and a stool completed the furnishings. He'd offered to buy a plastic play kitchen like the one in the commercials Katie had exclaimed over when they'd watched Saturday-morning cartoons last week. Jo had refused, insisting he'd done more than enough.

Now, reporter's notebook in hand, he surveyed the blacksmith shop—a barn, really—a hundred yards ahead. Across from the structure, a small cabin cozied up to a cluster of trees. Before he'd taken a step, a hound dog emerged from the woods and charged. Praying he wasn't the animal's next meal, he kept his eyes forward and strode toward the barn. The hound skidded to a halt, barked once, then fell in step with the visitor.

Sullivan paused inside the barn doorway, his eyes adjusting to the dim interior as he listened to the clanging metal and iron. Similar to Vulcan, the blacksmith of the gods, the clan blacksmith was larger than life. All muscle and brawn, Sullivan suspected this Vulcan could lay a man in his grave with one blow of a sledgehammer.

The dog woofed, announcing Sullivan's presence. The blacksmith set the tool aside. His red beard was spotted with gray and soot and his skin glistened with sweat, droplets beading on the thick mat of red fuzz carpeting his chest. As he drew nearer, Sullivan noted the man possessed open, honest, intelligent eyes. Unlike the character Joe Gargery in the Dickens novel *Great Expectations,* there was nothing strange or boorish about this iron worker.

"Sullivan Mooreland from Seattle, Washington." He extended his hand.

"Tom Kavenagh." The blacksmith's palm was huge—twice the size of Sullivan's—and as rough and thick as crocodile hide.

"We can talk while you work." Sullivan hoped to get the blacksmith to warm up to him before springing questions about Lightning Jack.

The heavy scent of ash, burning metal and smoke assaulted his nostrils. Dirt, dust and soot covered every surface, including the rough-hewn plank floor, which dipped in various places. An array of unidentifiable instruments hung from the walls and rafters. Stools, worktables and shelves, containing boxes of nails, tins and rusted buckets, cluttered one end of the building. The forge, or furnace, and an anvil occupied the middle space. A steel pipe ran from the chimney forge through the roof to draw the smoke outside—though Sullivan questioned its effectiveness. A huge monstrosity of metal and iron with a rubber belt and pulley system crowded the other end of the work space.

Kavenagh stopped in front of the forge, a rectangular brick structure, and puttered for a few moments, then motioned to a stool. "Sit a spell."

No sense arguing with 250 pounds of muscle. Sullivan made himself comfortable, flipped to a blank page in his notebook and licked the tip of his pen—an old habit that served no purpose but to leave a blue dot on the end of his tongue. "Mind if I jot down a few notes?"

Silence. Kavenagh's attention remained on the fire in the forge.

"Do you come from a long line of blacksmiths?"

The giant nodded but didn't elaborate.

"Spend most of your time repairing tools and shoeing horses?" Jo had informed Sullivan that Kavenagh's skills were famous throughout the mountains. A fair man who never overcharged for his services, the blacksmith was well respected for his artistic talent. He'd designed and made the scrollwork seen on many of the iron gates at the entrances to wealthy plantation estates throughout Kentucky.

"Ain't many horses left in the hollow, but I take care of 'em." Kavenagh placed a narrow bar of steel on the anvil, grasped a straight hammer and landed several blows to the metal before returning the object to the fire pit. "And I fix farm equipment. Mostly I work in my fields."

Jo had mentioned that Kavenagh farmed his land. "Any hobbies?"

"Make rockin' chairs during the winter months and sell 'em in tourist shops."

Before Sullivan had the chance to ask more about the chairs, Kavenagh began humming, his voice deep and gravelly. Sullivan suspected that working alone in a hot, noisy environment day after day made a man yearn for the sound of his own voice…anything other than the clang of metal and the roar of the furnace.

When Kavenagh finished the song, Sullivan asked, "What's the name of that tune?"

"'Soldier's Joy.' Sounds better on the banjo."

"Who taught you to play the banjo?"

"Taught myself. Growin' up, we always had callers stoppin' by. Lots of back-porch singin' and fiddlin'." He grinned, then shook his head.

"What?"

"Ma and her female friends would dance a few jigs. Shoot the Owl, Chase the Squirrel. Box the Gnat."

"You and your folks had an active social life."

"Nothing else to do in these woods 'cept sing, dance and drink. Had an uncle who played a mean clawstick and a cousin who could blow a straw. My mamaw played the washboard and papaw blew the jug."

"Are there any clan members who play those instruments today?"

Bushy eyebrows dipped. "Most youngins don't wanna learn the old instruments. They play them loud guitars and drums and scream the lyrics. Can't understand a dang word."

Evidently Jo wasn't the only clan member concerned about disappearing traditions.

"Mind givin' me a hand?" Kavenagh asked.

"Sure." Sullivan popped off the stool. "It's dark in here. How do you see what you're doing?"

"Got to be able to check the color of the metal." Kavenagh pointed to the glowing iron nestled in the embers. "That there yellow-orange is called forgin' heat. Means the iron's ready." He rested the bar on the anvil, then handed Sullivan a pair of pincers. "Hold steady."

Secure a two-foot-long wedge of metal with a pair of barbecue tongs while the giant pummeled one end…was the guy nuts? Sweat—the kind produced by nerves, not heat—broke out across Sullivan's brow when Kavenagh hefted an even bigger sledgehammer than the one he'd used earlier. With both hands he lifted the heavy mallet above his head, arm and neck muscles bulging under the weight.

The hammer came down, smashing the glowing tip dead-on. *Bam!* The steel Sullivan had been instructed to hold tight flew into the air, spinning front over end across the shop, where it embedded itself in the wall.

"Christ!" Sullivan's heart stalled out.

"Gotta hold it tighter 'n that," Kavenagh grumbled, then stomped over to the wall and worked the metal loose. The object had left a hole the size of a fist in the wood. He shoved the iron in the fire again, waited a minute, then transferred it to the anvil. "Try again."

This time Sullivan gripped the metal until his muscles ached. Twenty minutes passed with Sullivan holding and Kavenagh pounding. "How do you do this by yourself?" Sullivan asked when the piece went back into the fire for the third time.

"Use a lighter hammer and pound longer."

"How the hell do you bang iron all day and then work your farm?" Sullivan's arms and shoulders ached from exertion.

"Most days I don't work in the shop." After several more strikes, Kavenagh announced, "Finished."

"What is it?" Sullivan studied the twisted piece of metal.

"A gate latch."

"All that work for a piece of hardware you could have purchased from a store in Finnegan's Stand?"

"Waste of good money to pay fer somethin' I can make." Saving money aside, Sullivan suspected the big man found pleasure and satisfaction toiling in front of the forge.

Kavenagh's mind-set gave Sullivan an idea of what the clan's younger generation struggled with—why expend time and energy learning a trade such as blacksmithing, when the tools and products could be purchased for less money and half the time it took to make them?

"Thirsty?" Kavenagh asked.

"Can't feel my tongue." They walked to the cabin, where Sullivan examined one of the handmade rocking chairs on the porch after Kavenagh disappeared inside for drinks. A few minutes later the blacksmith stepped out of the house, carrying two tin cups and a pottery jug that would fetch top dollar at an antique auction. "Ale," he stated.

Sullivan sniffed the light amber liquid. A floral peaty aroma. He held the cup in the air and toasted, "Long live the forge."

In one swallow, the blacksmith downed the drink, then made a hissing sound. Sullivan sipped his, letting the spicy herbal flavor roll across his tongue before swallowing. "Did you make this or buy it from Lightning Jack?" Sullivan watched Kavenagh's face, but there was no reaction to the bootlegger's name.

"What interest you got in Lightning Jack?"

"I hope to interview him for a story. The notorious moonshiner is a national legend."

With a frown, Kavenagh argued, "Most bootleggers don't confess to makin' moonshine."

"Is this the same stuff Jo brews?" When Kavenagh's eyes narrowed, he added, "I've seen Jo's still. She claims she makes whiskey for the clan."

"Jo's the only one who knows her grandfather's secret recipe."

"Secret recipe?"

"Her kinfolk settled these mountains. Her ancestors brewed for the king of Scotland. The recipe for ale comes straight from the king's table."

Jo was a generous, caring woman and he suspected she'd do anything to help her clan. He didn't want to believe she would knowingly break the law, but why would she spend so much time at a task that took her away from Katie in the middle of the night—*unless she had no other choice.* He remembered that she'd mentioned giving up a teaching position in Finnegan's Stand. She probably didn't earn as much instructing the kids in the hollow. "Does she sell the ale illegally?"

"Why would she do a dang-fool thing like that?"

"Money." Now that he thought about it, he wondered if Jo even charged tuition to attend her school.

"The clan folk do a lot of tradin' and borrowin' with one another. I give her corn and potatoes and she gives me ale."

"If it's all on the up-and-up, why does she make moonshine in the dead of night?"

Without missing a beat, Kavenagh explained, "'Cause it's part of the recipe."

"Huh?"

"You gotta make moonshine under the cover of darkness or you jinx the flavor."

Are you kidding me? Sounded phony to Sullivan, but what did he know about anything in these mountains—only what he'd read in books. And a book was one author's interpretation.

An idea began to *brew* in Sullivan's mind. Supporting his feature story on Lightning Jack would be a bigger, broader, more sweeping saga—the disappearing Scotch-Irish clan of Heather's Hollow.

Chapter Eight

"Who have you arranged for me to talk to today?" Sullivan asked Jo Saturday morning when she met him at the cabin door.

Darn. She must have dreamed that wild animals had dragged the reporter into the woods overnight. His hair stuck up on end and blond beard stubble covered his face. Sexy— even in rumpled clothes, there was no other adjective to describe Sullivan's fresh-from-bed appeal. "You're stuck with me," she grumbled. After his visit with the clan blacksmith a few days ago, she'd hoped Sullivan would give up on his mission and pack his bags. Instead he'd spent the past two days doing research on the school computers—for what, he wouldn't say. At least he'd been preoccupied and she hadn't had to worry about returning home and discovering him constructing a carport for her.

The memory of Sullivan building a tree house for Katie still tweaked at Jo's heart. The sweet gesture made it difficult to remain miffed with the man. Not that she had time for such emotions. The school year had officially ended two weeks ago and she'd used every one of her fourteen days allowed to file student-information forms with the Kentucky State Department of Education. Now that she'd finished the task, she'd spend the remainder of the summer revising the curriculum, learning a new literacy software program targeted for the younger students' language development and increasing her production of moonshine.

None of that would happen if Sullivan hung around much
longer. "Before anyone does any more interviewing, I've go
errands to do in town," she announced.

"Great. I'll tag along and make a call to my boss."

"Katie's upstairs dressing. Bathroom's yours." She un
hooked the screen latch, then retreated to the kitchen, ignoring
the soft tread of her enemy's shoes across the floor and the quie
click of the bathroom door. *Enemy?* Yeah, right. If Sullivan ir
ritated her so much, why did her pulse jump each morning
when he stood on the porch smiling at her?

Hearing the water pipes rattle, Jo scrubbed the counter, hoping
to wipe out the image of Sullivan naked in the tub. She threw the
rag in the sink, collected the stack of bills and letters for the pos
office, then made a grocery list, before hollering, "Put som
scoot in your boot, Katie. We're leaving in ten minutes."

Outside on the porch, Jo studied the drooping flowers in th
pots. She'd watered those yesterday—or had it been the da
before? *Good grief.* Since Sullivan had dropped in for a visit, he
daily routine had been flipped on end. Speaking of unwanted re
porters... Sullivan stepped out of the house, wearing a fresh
short-sleeved golf shirt and a pair of khaki pants. His scuffed shoe
with a ragged tear near the big toe completed his *reporter* persona

"I'm down to my last pair of boxers," he stated. "Mind if
use your washer and dryer later?"

A boxers man. She wished he hadn't mentioned his under
wear. Tonight she'd dream of him wearing boxers instead of
towel as he sprinted from Shotgun Granny.

Ignoring the sexy way his damp hair curled over his shi
collar, she inquired, "Haven't you had enough of all this?" Sh
swept her arm through the air.

"No way. Listen, Jo." He crept closer and she caught a whiff of men's cologne. A heavy, musky scent that made her yearn to suck in a deep breath and hold it until her lungs burst. "I've given a lot of thought to what you've been telling me."

"I've told you a lot of things. Which subject in particular are you referring to?"

"You implied that if my story focuses solely on Lightning Jack and his infamous moonshining, I'll misrepresent the clan's culture."

"Oh." At the moment—with Sullivan's minty breath puffing in her face, Jo wasn't capable of a more coherent response.

"Kavenagh mentioned that the younger generation isn't carrying on the clan traditions." Sullivan shoved a hand through his wet hair, leaving the top of his head looking like a freshly plowed field. "I'll check with my boss, but I'm positive I can help."

Good Lord, the last thing she wanted was a reporter's assistance.

"I won't focus solely on Lightning Jack. I'll include the whole clan." His brown eyes glittered with excitement. "America's disappearing culture—the Scotch-Irish of the Appalachians."

His enthusiasm sent Jo to the opposite end of the porch, where she inhaled a lungful of mountain air to clear her head of Sullivan's lingering scent. "I don't—"

"Wait," he interrupted. "With your educational background and interest in teaching the younger generation the importance of their heritage, you're the perfect person to rescue the clan from extinction."

Extinction? "We're not a bunch of rare Amazon tree frogs that need saving."

"The publicity from my story could be your big break." His fervor was palpable and Jo focused on remaining calm.

"We don't want federal agencies interfering or insisting they know how to save us from ourselves." She crossed her arms over her chest—a habit when she felt threatened. "Health investigators will take one gander at Granny's jar of leeches, then institutionalize her. Education professionals will shut down my classroom and force the kids to return to the school in Finnegan's Stand. DEA agents will swarm the woods destroying stills and—"

"Don't be so dramatic," he scolded.

"Ready, Mama," her daughter stated before Jo had a chance to defend herself. Katie smiled. "'Mornin', Mr. Sully."

"Good morning, Katie."

Jo had never met a man who lit a fire under her the way Sullivan did. Yet for all his frustrating quirks, she enjoyed sparring with him. Yep, she'd definitely miss arguing with him after he left for Seattle. As she straightened her daughter's hair bow, she announced, "Let's hit the road." Sullivan jogged ahead to the truck and opened the passenger-side door for Katie.

By the time Jo drove down the mountain and parked in front of the post office in Finnegan's Stand, she wanted to pound knots on Sullivan's noggin. The man knew zip about kids. No sane adult would encourage a child to sing at the top of her lungs in a moving vehicle.

A hundred cups of ale on the wall…a hundred cups of ale… If Katie hadn't been so tickled, Jo would have put an end to the nonsense. But her daughter basked in Sullivan's attention. Until now, Jo hadn't considered how the absence of a man in Katie's life would affect the child in the long run—not that she believed Sullivan would make a suitable father for her daughter. He acted more like a playmate than a parental figure.

Don't be hard on the man, Jo. He's patient and kind. Katie likes him. And how many times have you heard the two joking and laughing together? She slid from the driver's seat, then helped her daughter out of the truck.

"Can I go with Mr. Sully. Please, Mama?"

"I don't mind." Sullivan patted Katie's red curls. "She can be my sentry when I'm on the phone."

Blue eyes rounded and Katie's voice edged with childlike awe. "What's a sentry?"

"You'll make a better one than the McKee boys," Sullivan mumbled.

Katie gazed at Sullivan as if he was her hero and for an instant panic seized Jo. How would her daughter react when the reporter got his story, said his goodbyes and disappeared? Jo was a big girl. She'd survive. But Katie's young, impressionable heart would break. "Maybe you should come with—"

"We'll be fine. I'll keep an eye on her," Sullivan insisted.

Shocked, Jo witnessed Katie slide her hand into Sullivan's. Anyone would easily mistake them for father and daughter. Throat aching, Jo squeezed out the words, "Behave yourself, young lady." Then she kissed her daughter's cheek and the pair walked off.

Not only did Jo have to fret over her growing feelings for Sullivan, but now she had to worry over her daughter's emotional state when the reporter left the hollow for good. And there was no doubt in her mind, Sullivan would leave.

The only question was…when?

"BE REAL QUIET, Katie." Sullivan pressed a finger to his lips as he lifted the telephone receiver and punched in the code on his calling card.

"Okay, Mr. Sully." Arms wrapped around his leg, Katie sat on Sullivan's shoe.

Little traffic zipped through Finnegan's Stand, and he doubted child abductions were rampant in the area. Even though he suspected mountain people had eyes in the backs of their heads and saw everything, he planned to make sure Katie didn't slip away while he was preoccupied on the phone. In order to extract her promise not to budge, he had to agree to give her a ride on his shoe to the café for ice cream after the call.

"Howard, it's Sullivan," he said, when the editor-in-chief picked up.

"About time you checked in. How's the story coming? Get the interview yet?"

Worried Katie might overhear the conversation and repeat it to Jo, Sullivan glanced down, relieved that the kid was more interested in tying his shoestrings together than eavesdropping. "About the interview..." he began.

"Can't find the bootlegger?"

Crap. Nothing slipped past the chief. "Lightning Jack's gone underground and there's no telling when the geezer will surface. But I intend to stick around awhile longer and check a few more leads," he lied, knowing darn well there wasn't any lead left to check.

"My patience is running out, Mooreland. You've got one more week to get the story. If you don't, you'll be using vacation time until your ass is back at your desk. Understand?"

"Yeah. Howard, this clan is fascinating." Not to mention the woman with a cause too big for her slim shoulders. "I plan to focus not only on Lightning Jack but on the disappearing culture of the Scotch-Irish—"

Laughter interrupted Sullivan's spiel. "America's bursting with disappearing cultures. People don't care about a bunch of rowdy, illiterate mountain people."

It was this narrow-minded view that Jo struggled against every day, that Sullivan intended to change with his story. "You're wrong, Howard. I can make people care." Out of the corner of his eye, he saw a flash of red drive past. He glanced up in time to see the tail end of his Corvette turn the corner and disappear from sight. "Wait!" he shouted.

"Wait for what?" Howard barked.

"Boss, my instincts are good. This story has the potential to be big. National big. Recognition for the paper."

"This time I'm listening to *my* instincts. One week, then you're on your own time."

"But…" The Corvette whizzed by again with a different front-seat passenger. The driver, a cross between a Hells Angel and Santa Claus, waved at Sullivan the second time around. "Stop!" He shook his fist in the air and dragged his Katie foot as far as the phone cord allowed. "Stop nothing! Get the story or else—"

Distracted by the carjacker, Sullivan snapped, "Or else what, Howard?"

"You can kiss that promotion goodbye." *Click.*

Jeez, his boss had been cranky.

"Ice cream?" Katie asked.

"Yep." Keeping his eyes peeled for the Corvette, he walked Katie to the café three doors down from the pay phone. "Okay, ride's up."

"That was fun, Mr. Sully, thanks." She scrambled from his shoe.

"My pleasure." Inside, a few customers gossiped over coffee at two of the tables. He and Katie grabbed stools at the counter. A scowling Betty Sue materialized out of thin air. "Where's your mama, Katie?" she asked, eyes narrowing on Sullivan.

"Post office. Mr. Sully's gonna buy me ice cream."

"Is that right…Mr. Sully?"

"I'm watching Katie until her mother catches up with us," he explained.

"What flavor is it gonna be?" The large-boned woman posed the question to Katie.

"Strawberry, please. And can I have a cherry on top?"

"Absolutely, sweetie." Betty Sue quirked an eyebrow at Sullivan.

"Chocolate. With a cherry, too."

The waitress rolled her eyes, then disappeared into the kitchen. While they waited, Sullivan shifted on the stool so he had a view of the street through the front window.

"Here ya go." Two bowls of ice cream clunked against the counter.

"Hey, Betty Sue. Who's driving the red Corvette?"

"That would be Amos. Charges fifty cents a spin," she added, then grabbed the coffeepot and headed for the other patrons.

Sullivan didn't know whether to laugh or yell. The last thing he wanted was an old fart driving his car into a ditch.

"Mr. Sully?"

Katie's voice broke his train of thought and he momentarily forgot the car. "What?"

"Do you like my mama?" Saucer-shaped eyes blinked.

In case Betty Sue's big ears were tuned in to their conversation, he lowered his voice. "Your mother's—" *Stubborn. Beautiful. Sexy.* "A real nice lady."

"'Cause sometimes I see her starin' out the window."

"Lots of people stare out windows."

"Nah." Katie elbowed him in the thigh. "Mama never did until you came."

Jo was spying on the cookhouse at night? Did she dream about joining him...on that table? Speaking of tables... "Maybe you can sneak me an extra blanket. My bed is awfully hard."

"Okay. Mr. Sully?"

How long did it take to mail a few letters?

"If Mama says it's okay, do you wanna be my daddy?"

Oh, boy. He should have never built the tree house. He

hadn't considered that it might put ideas in the little girl's head—ideas that wouldn't result in one big happy family.

"Well, Katie, the whole daddy thing is kind of complicated."

"It is?" Her mouth formed an O.

The elf's expression—confusion mixed with hope—pulled at Sullivan's heart. "Your mother can probably explain—"

"Explain what?" Jo walked out of the kitchen at the café. How long had she stood behind the door, listening?

"I asked Mr. Sully if he can be my daddy."

Jo's gaze pinned Sullivan. "And what did Mr. Sully say?"

"It's conkcli…compkla…"

"Complicated," Sullivan said for the child, shifting under the weight of her mother's suspicious glare.

"Finish your ice cream, Katie. Mr. Mooreland and I are going outside for a minute."

Mr. Mooreland? He must be in big trouble. He followed Jo out of the café, noting the soft sway of her hips in too-tight jeans. Being Katie's daddy would certainly come with a few perks. As soon as the door shut behind him, Jo embedded a finger in his chest.

"Don't fill my daughter's head with happy-ever-after stories."

"I didn't, Jo." He held up his hands. "Katie invited me to be her daddy and I told her she'd better talk to you."

The fire in her eyes fizzled.

"Has Katie been wondering about her father?" he pried.

"Yes." Jo plucked her finger from his breastbone. "She understands Brian won't ever be a part of our lives, but she hopes I'll find a new father for her and a husband for me." Jo's lips curved. "And she says it's okay if they aren't the same man."

He chuckled, then his thoughts sobered. "You said you didn't want a man in your life." The idea of Jo and some lumberjack guy naked in a bed—or naked anywhere—irritated Sullivan like a nagging cough. If he hadn't kissed Jo, caressed her breasts, felt her body rub his, he'd never experience another man's treasure.

"Relax, Sullivan, I'm not on the make. I doubt I'll ever marry."

"Why?"

"Because I intend to live here the rest of my life."

For some reason he felt compelled to contest her decision. "You're saying if the perfect man came along, you wouldn't marry him unless he agreed to live in Heather's Hollow?" Silence crowded the scant space between them.

"The right man wouldn't ask me to leave my home," Jo stated.

If that wasn't a challenge, Sullivan didn't know what was.

"MIND IF I…" Sullivan nodded to the mound of dirty laundry in his arms as he climbed the steps to the cabin.

Jo had been sitting in the rocking chair for the past hour, perusing a software manual while Katie played in the tree house. She hadn't made much progress, her thoughts continually straying to Sullivan and their discussion about her marriage goals at Scooter's Café. "Help yourself. The machines are on the back porch."

"The noise won't bother you?"

Was Sullivan always this considerate? *Probably.* "Nope."

Nodding to the book in her hand, he asked, "Interesting reading?"

"I think so. Why?"

His mouth spread…showcasing the sexy dimple in his cheek. "Because I'm next in line for your undivided attention." He disappeared inside the house, this time leaving her whopperjawed. Ten minutes later, he reappeared.

"Took you long enough. Decide to use the washboard instead of the machine?" she teased.

"Ha, ha." He sat in the rocker next to her. "I learned how to use a washing machine when I was Katie's age."

"Why so young?" Sullivan knew more about her than she knew about him—the trademark of a good reporter, she suspected. Learn everything about your subject without revealing anything about yourself.

"If my mother wasn't at a job she was either in a bar or passed out on the couch. One day a neighborhood bully threatened to beat me and I wet my pants."

Jo pictured a little boy with tears in his big brown eyes, running from a mean brat.

"I didn't have any clean underwear for school the next day, so I stuffed my clothes into a plastic grocery sack and marched down the block to the Laundromat on the corner. I didn't understand I had to pay to wash my clothes. A guy covered in tattoos handed me a few quarters and taught me how to run the machines."

"You're lucky that man didn't abduct you." She shuddered at the idea of leaving Katie alone in a launderette.

"The guy was cool. We talked about his motorcycle and he folded my clothes. And then he gave me pointers on how to handle the bully."

"Pointers?"

"Kick him in the crotch and run." Sullivan chuckled. "Before the dude left, he handed over his remaining quarters and told me to hide them in a safe place for next time."

Her mother's heart ached as she imagined a miniature Sullivan, barely tall enough to open a machine lid. "Were you left to fend for yourself often?" He owed her a few answers in return for room and board, making a nuisance of himself and reminding her on a daily basis that she was attracted to him.

"Yeah. I never understood why my mother kept me around when she could have put me up for adoption or farmed me out to foster care."

"She must have loved you." Jo doubted Sullivan heard her. His gaze remained riveted on the cookhouse across the yard, probably reliving a memory from the past. She raised her voice. "Despite your challenging childhood, you became a success."

He blinked, then squirmed in his chair. "That depends on how you define *success.*"

Lord, the man was tough on himself. "You can't deny you've done well for yourself."

"I've done all right. Now I need to convince my boss that success earned the old-fashioned way—hard work and self-sacrifice—is enough to promote me."

"A college education doesn't automatically make you deserving, never mind intelligent."

"You *earned* a college degree," he argued.

"Yes, but I'm no better than the next person. For years, outsiders have mocked our clan, claiming we're ignorant because many of us, especially the older generation, chose not to attend college or pursue a formal education beyond middle school. I don't judge people based on their education, but on their intentions, honesty, work ethic and values. Who cares if a person—" Jo ceased ranting when Sullivan opened his notepad and scribbled on a page. "What are you doing?"

"Taking notes."

Trying to ignore the pain in her chest at the realization Sullivan had wanted her undivided attention because he'd intended to discuss Lightning Jack and the clan, and not because he'd wanted to cuddle or smooch with her, she protested, "I didn't agree to an interview."

"Don't worry, I won't publish your name." His eyes glowed with excitement. "And I won't ask you for secret moonshine recipes, but help me understand the allure that surrounds bootlegging in the Appalachians."

What could it hurt to chat with him? Often her discussions about the clan's heritage were with people who didn't care, or with her students and their wandering minds. At least Sullivan's interest was genuine. Maybe after she pacified his curiosity she might persuade him to focus his attention on *her.* "I'm sure you already know that in the late-nineteenth and early-twentieth centuries, manufacturing illegal whiskey was a means of earning cash in a subsistence economy. Over time bootlegging evolved into a large secretive presence in the mountain culture," Jo explained.

"Why?"

"I can't speak for other clans in the area, only ours. Most of us are deeply religious and believe that social drinking shouldn't be encouraged. Those who are determined to drink usually do so in private or with their close friends. The clan doesn't condone public intoxication." A queasiness gripped Jo's intestines. What a hypocrite she was—preaching about religious beliefs and attitudes toward liquor consumption when she knowingly went against her clan's moral code by brewing heather whiskey.

"Then wouldn't members of the clan consider moonshiners criminals?"

Until Jo had begun making moonshine, she hadn't considered how harsh a word *criminal* was. "Not in the way common drug dealers are. Most neighbors are on friendly terms with former moonshiners." She gathered her thoughts, then continued. "Home brewing is in the blood and has been an important part of our clan's history for centuries. It's more than making whiskey or passing down a family recipe—it's a way of honoring our past and never forgetting each generation's fight to retain our clan's independence from outside influence."

"Then why not establish a legal brewery? A place to carry on the traditions within the limits of the law?"

"Because breaking the law has historically been our clan's way of snubbing authority."

"What about taxes? Why should bootleggers be exempt?"

"The clan doesn't receive government assistance, so we feel

no obligation to pay." *And I need every penny to support the school and my daughter.*

"How many clan members work their own stills?"

Her heart insisted she could trust him, but her mind argued he was a flatlander, using the clan to further his career. "Not as many as you'd believe. When the sawmill opened forty years ago, most of the men hired on there. With steady hours and a weekly paycheck, there was neither time nor the necessity to make whiskey."

"Did clan members make moonshine runs during the 1920's or '30s?"

"I don't recall hearing any stories," she lied. With a pang of sadness, Jo remembered sitting on her grandfather's knee, listening to his tales about accompanying his father on whiskey runs to Chicago and Atlanta during Prohibition. Her grandfather had been very clever in avoiding the law. Never once had he been arrested—a feat most bootleggers couldn't boast of.

"What about Lightning Jack? Did he do his own driving or hire someone?" Sullivan flipped to a blank page in his notebook, then studied Jo with an intensity that gave her pause.

Jo caved in to the expectant expression on Sullivan's face. "As the story goes, Lightning Jack's grandfather taught him how to make moonshine at the age of seven. When he turned thirteen, he drove his first delivery."

"That's a lot of responsibility for a teen."

"Made perfect sense to use younger boys to transport moonshine. If they got busted by the law, they went to jail for a few hours and were released to their mothers. This way the fathers and grandfathers stayed out of trouble and continued to make whiskey and work their farms."

"Did Lightning Jack drink the stuff he made?"

"The moonshiner's rule has been passed down from father

to son for generations in our clan—This Stuff Is For Selling, Not Drinking."

"Has anyone in the clan ever revealed the identity of a bootlegger to the law?"

"Not that I'm aware." And Jo was trying desperately to hold to the clan's code of silence. She added, "Our survival hinges upon the general attitude of us against the outside world."

"Is that mentality alive and well today?"

Their talk was sounding more and more akin to an interview and not a discussion. "To some extent. But we need to find common ground among us regarding the future. The old-timers rebel against change, and the younger generation demand that the clan catch up with the rest of the world."

Tap, tap, tap. Jo sensed Sullivan's frustration building. "Why would a member of the clan respect someone who breaks the law and doesn't pay his taxes? What kind of an example is that for the younger generation?"

"The bootlegger is a product of his community. Lightning Jack may break certain social mores, but he strongly adheres to the values of the clan, albeit in an unconventional manner."

"How so?"

"He lends a hand to neighbors in crisis. He's fiercely protective of his family. He's religious—doesn't always attend church regularly, but he can quote Scripture and he slows down out of respect when he drives by a house of worship. Even though he quit school after the fourth grade, he respects knowledge and encourages kids to get an education."

"Sounds as if he's a good man."

"Lightning Jack has what we call *worth.* He may have been a little wild in his day and many people might not approve of his bootlegging, but because of his personal values, he has worth. He's earned our respect."

"The man—"

"Wait," Jo interrupted, "I'm not finished. Lighting Jack never relied on anyone to make his living, nor did he allow anyone to dictate what he could or couldn't do to make money to support his family. That's an important trait of our clan."

"The bootlegger personifies an antihero. No wonder books and movies have romanticized moonshining."

"What people don't see, Sullivan, is the other side to moonshining. Bootleggers don't pay taxes, but none of them lives extravagantly. They sell only what they require to support their families. Leftovers are handed out to neighbors for medicinal purposes or given to those who can't afford to pay." *And the profits from Lightning Jack's still paid for my college education. How can that be wrong?*

"The clan may consider Lightning Jack a noble man, but there's no guarantee the rest of society will view him that way," Sullivan argued.

"That's why it's important for the younger generation to understand their roots."

"Maybe you've got it wrong, Jo. Maybe it's not the kids who have to understand but the rest of the world." His gaze pinned her. "And the only way you'll accomplish that task is to leave the life you're fighting to preserve."

Chapter Nine

"'Leave the life I'm trying to preserve'?" Jo muttered as she dressed for church in the bathroom while Sullivan and Katie ate breakfast. Since yesterday, when he'd made the comment, Jo had wallowed in a self-induced angstfest.

Did he expect her to travel the country, lecturing at universities and colleges—as if talk would change opinions and treatment of her clan? *Yeah, right.* She loved Heather's Hollow and proposed to fight her battle from the comfort of her schoolhouse.

Chicken.

Darn right she was jumpy. Her experience with Brian had taught her a hard-learned lesson—never trust a flatlander.

Sullivan's different. His intentions are honorable and worthy.

Maybe to a certain extent. She believed the reporter genuinely wanted to help in her quest to save the traditions of the clan. But that was because he had a stake in Jo's cause. Recognition. Fame. A promotion.

"Blasted curls." *Pat, pat. Boing, boing.* She studied her reflection in the mirror. Since when had she cared about her appearance?

Since Sullivan. Since you decided you liked him—a lot.

She understood Sullivan on a deeper level and admired that he was as passionate and dedicated to his cause as she was to hers. Not that a newspaper feature story compared with educating an entire generation of youth. She gave up on the curls. Brian had done a real number on her. Until Sullivan happened along, Jo hadn't acknowledged the depth of her first lover's cut.

You're a very pretty woman, Johanna Macpherson.

As she mulled over Sullivan's flattery, she searched for a hint of insincerity but found none. Despite her resolve to sail through life as a single mother, her reaction to his compliment proved she hadn't succeeded in burying her feminine desires. A part of her yearned for the love of a man. A partner in life to help shoulder the responsibility of raising her daughter. A soul mate who would support her goals.

Why Sullivan? Why another flatlander—someone who didn't understand her culture? He deserves a chance.

From the beginning, he'd made his intentions clear—to wow the world with an exposé of Lightning Jack. He'd been honest about his motivation—the editor job. Then, after his visit with Tom Kavenagh, Sullivan had adjusted his thinking and had decided his feature article should focus on both Lightning Jack and the clan's struggle to preserve their traditions.

Trading in certain success for a commentary on the struggles of a Scotch-Irish clan unknown to most of America didn't make sense. Did she dare hope Sullivan cared more about her than he let on?

Part of her resented his interference. He'd made her question the path she'd chosen to help her people. She'd been positive educating the youth was the best way, but Sullivan had brought up a good point, one she'd purposefully refused to consider— that the outside world also needed to be educated.

The prospect of standing on a stage for the world to critique, criticize or, worse, pity scared the bejesus out of her. She'd been laughed at and ridiculed enough for one lifetime, why subject herself to more? *For the children, Jo.* She didn't want those in the younger generation to grow up and find themselves in the same painful, humiliating position Brian had put her in.

As if a round of buckshot had exploded in Jo's gut, guilt peppered her insides. All these years she'd convinced herself that if she could prevent the clan's world from changing, she and Katie would remain safe. Is that how she wished her daughter to live life—afraid of everything and anyone not from the hollow? One day Katie would decide to find her own place in the world. What right did Jo have to pick that place for her daughter?

Angry with herself, she glared at her reflection. Why couldn't it have been her grandfather or Granny—anyone but a flatlander—to open her eyes?

No matter how she wished to remain angry with Sullivan, she couldn't. Good Lord, she'd sent the man on a wild-goose chase to Tennessee. He'd had his breakfast doctored with stool mover. He'd been forced to sleep on a table. He'd been held prisoner by a shotgun-toting granny. And he'd had to be rescued from a tree. If anyone had a reason to feel humiliated and embarrassed, it was Sullivan. Amazingly the man swallowed his pride and kept going after what he wanted.

That's because he's alone in the world. He doesn't have to worry how his actions affect others. Sullivan's aloneness bothered Jo. He'd acted as though he hadn't cared that his few personal relationships with women hadn't lasted long, yet she'd caught the note of loneliness in his voice. She suspected the man wasn't even aware of his desire for companionship.

Part of her yearned to be that one special person he shared his innermost secrets with. Not one to vocalize her hopes and wishes, Jo believed she could trust him with her dreams. No matter how at odds she and Sullivan were with each other, he respected her mission and would never knowingly jeopardize her cause.

"Ready, Mama," Katie called. The bang of the screen door followed her outside.

Saved from overanalyzing her relationship with Sullivan, she cast one last glance in the mirror. After checking the buttons on the front of her dress, she opened the bathroom door.

"Wow." Sullivan's appreciative gaze lingered on the dress's gathered bodice before sliding down the rest of her body. Heat surged through Jo, snatching her breath. Leaving her toes tingling.

"If you don't mind—" Sullivan cleared his throat "—I'd like to tag along to church. Afterwards I'll take you two ladies for a spin in my Corvette."

The words were cocky, but his earnest expression hinted at his wish to be included in her and Katie's Sunday ritual. She supposed it wouldn't hurt to return his car. He'd already discovered the still. And it had been too long—years, in fact—since she'd gone for an afternoon drive with a handsome man.

"Please, Jo." The dimple in his cheek winked at her.

"Katie would enjoy a ride." When she made a move for the door, he blocked her path.

"And would Katie's mother appreciate a ride in my Corvette?" Brown eyes darkened.

"Yes." Embarrassed that her answer sighed from her mouth, she glanced away.

He held the screen door open. "Good thing we're headed to church first."

"Why's that?" She paused at his side.

"Because I should ask for forgiveness in advance," he murmured, his lips brushing her ear.

"Forgiveness for what?"

"The sin I plan to commit with you today."

HEATHER HOLLOW Presbyterian Church sat on the banks of Periwinkle Creek, high above the town of Finnegan's Stand. The traditional white-clapboard structure had a double door at the front of the building, three stained-glass windows on each side and a small steeple pointing heavenward. Eleven vehicles—twelve, counting Jo's truck—occupied the dirt lot adjacent to the building.

Next to the church, enclosed within a faded-to-gray-in-places white picket fence, snuggled a cemetery against the hillside. As if they were the eyes of heaven, small gray headstones dotted the green grass. Organ music greeted Sullivan's ears when they got out of the truck.

"We're late. We'll have to sit in the rear," Jo explained, grabbing Katie's hand and tugging her toward the stone steps. He followed, his hand against the feminine curve of Jo's back. He wasn't sure if the gesture was meant to offer her support or him. He'd never been in a church for a service and doubted he'd be welcomed by God.

The scent of lemon oil tickled his nose when he entered the sanctuary. Their footfalls clacked against the plank floor as Jo slipped into the second pew from the door. They remained standing—Jo joining in the singing. Katie scooted past her mother to retrieve the hymnal resting at the end of the bench. Sullivan noted most of the churchgoers carried their own Bibles, and none used the hymnal but sang from memory.

A woman pastor stood behind the pulpit, her voice joining the congregation in song. A quick count turned up twenty-one worshippers—including him, Jo and Katie. Not a full house by any means. They were middle-aged people and older. Katie was the only child present.

Song after song, the singing continued—the hymns slow and devoid of any regular beat. After a few stanzas he discovered each person added his or her own twist to the song. The woman across the aisle held the last note longest. The man in front of Sullivan stretched the O's. Jo clipped the end of her words. The variations created a unique sound.

By the fourth hymn Sullivan's knees ached and he wished

he could sit with Katie in the pew and help her count the polka dots on her dress. Finally the song ended and the pastor motioned for everyone to sit. With a cherry-cheeked smile, she bid the parishioners welcome, her gaze ferreting Sullivan out in the gathering. He suspected he had the appearance of a man who'd never worshiped regularly.

"Fiona Seamus is our pastor," Jo whispered in his ear. "Her husband works at the mill."

The explanation was drowned in the waves of Jo's scent— today a mix of flowers and spice. For a moment, Sullivan forgot he sat in the Lord's house and lost himself in Jo and the shining red curls that cascaded over her shoulders. He ached to tangle his hands in the strands—their silkiness forever embedded in his fingertips.

Her blue-and-green patterned dress gathered beneath her breasts, emphasizing their lushness. Her legs were bare, the creamy whiteness of her skin dotted with delicate freckles. When he imagined cataloging and kissing those tiny specks on other parts of her body, his pants became uncomfortably tight.

Embarrassed by his lustful musings in the Lord's house, Sullivan forced himself to pay attention to the sermon, which promoted goodwill on earth. Two hymns and twenty minutes later, the pastor closed the service with a prayer for the clan's safekeeping. The parishioners waited for the pastor to reach the door before standing and exiting the pews.

"What about the collection?" Sullivan asked Jo.

"We don't pay our pastors."

"Why not?"

She lowered her voice. "Preachers and pastors are expected to make their own way in the world. The clan has always believed a person doesn't require a seminary education or credentials to become a pastor, because that kind of instruction is no substitute for spiritual inspiration and insight.

"Fiona, this is Sullivan Mooreland," Jo said upon reaching the pastor. "He's visiting from Seattle, Washington."

"Welcome to the hollow, Mr. Mooreland."

"Enjoyed the sermon, Pastor Seamus." Sullivan shook her hand. Relief filled him when the woman's interest returned to Jo.

"I'd hoped to invite Katie over to bake cookies after church today, but I forgot to call."

Katie bounced from one foot to the other. "Can I go, Mama? Can I?"

Say yes, Jo.

The pastor's eyes narrowed on Sullivan and he dropped his gaze to his shoes, praying—since this was the closest he'd ever get to God—that the woman wasn't psychic and knew he had sinning on his mind.

"Sure," Jo agreed.

Yes!

"Sullivan and I have errands to run," Jo explained. If she wanted to call joyriding an errand, who was he to disagree?

"Take your time. We'll find things to do, won't we?" The pastor smiled at Katie.

"Mind Mrs. Seamus, honey."

"Okay, Mama."

Jo kissed her daughter's cheek, and with a wave, Katie disappeared inside the church with the pastor.

Sullivan followed Jo to the truck, where she removed a bouquet of fresh-picked flowers tied with a yellow ribbon. Motioning to the graveyard, she said, "I'll be quick."

Curious, he followed at a respectable distance, not wishing to invade her privacy but interested in discovering who the flowers were for. The haphazard rows of headstones reminded him that he wasn't able to visit his mother's final resting place because she'd been cremated and her ashes dumped in the ocean. Not that it mattered where his mother was. He'd had little to say to her on a good day.

"Join me if you like," Jo invited him at the gate.

With a few brisk steps he closed the distance between them. They meandered along a path curving around the headstones— a few brand-new and polished, others tilted at odd angles, stained and dirty with names and dates unreadable. They hiked several yards up the hill at the rear of the grassy plot until they arrived at a lone stub of granite high above the cemetery, facing the pristine valley below. Heather surrounded the marker on three sides.

"The view has that effect on everyone." Jo smiled.

Confused, he muttered, "What effect?"

Tapping the end of her finger against the underside of his chin, she murmured, "Your mouth was hanging open."

"I've never seen anything so peaceful. Not even the ocean compares with the serenity of this spot."

"Grandpa asked to be buried here because he wanted to watch over the clan and the hollow." Jo placed the bouquet in front of the headstone, which was commanding in its simplicity and insignificant size.

Robert McCulley 1910–2005. Inscribed below the name— *Creag Dhu.* Pointing to the words, he asked, "What's that?"

In a heavy Gaelic accent, Jo read the words, then added, "It's the clan war cry."

"Does it translate into English?"

She explained, "It's the name of a rock in the neighborhood of Cluny Castle in Scotland, our motherland."

Sullivan chuckled. "That must have been something to hear a band of fierce warriors shout a rock's name before attacking." Turning serious, he added, "I would have enjoyed meeting your grandfather, Jo."

"He loved to tell stories. Katie was only four when he died

and doesn't remember much about him, save for the times he sat her on his knee and spun tales about fairies, leprechauns and pots of gold."

"You miss him, don't you?"

"Yes. I was close to my grandfather. He believed in my school and in my goal to keep the younger generation from leaving the hollow."

Sullivan moved off, allowing her privacy. He followed the path through the headstones until he reached the gate, then hesitated. His chest tightened at the picture Jo made at the top of the hill. The wind lifting her hair off her shoulders, the proud tilt of her chin as she gazed over the terrain. He imagined her dressed as a warrior ready to defend her clan to the death. If he hadn't understood before, he realized now that Jo was a part of this land, its people and its history.

Where did he belong? Nowhere. Shaking off the thought, he continued toward the truck. Five minutes later, Jo appeared and without a word they drove from the church.

"Still interested in going for that spin?" she asked.

"I haven't changed my mind, have you?"

"No." They made the trip to town in silence, a subtle tension building between them. Once they entered Finnegan's Stand, she turned onto the main street and cruised past the businesses to the end of the road, where she entered a winding dirt path. Up ahead, Sullivan spotted an old gristmill—and his Corvette.

Before the truck had come to a complete stop, he jumped out and circled the car. He'd expected to find scratches, dents and smashed fries on the seats. Instead he discovered the vehicle was in perfect condition—as if it had been washed and waxed moments earlier. Even the hubcaps twinkled in the sun.

A barrel-chested man rounded the corner of the building. Sullivan recognized him as the joyrider who'd driven the car through town. Jo hugged the bearded man.

"Amos, this is Sullivan Mooreland, the owner of the Corvette."

"Mighty fine vehicle ya got there, mister." Amos stuck a beefy hand out. "Hums like a satisfied woman."

How could Sullivan stay angry with a man who obviously appreciated fine machinery. He doubted Amos would ever own anything as fancy and useless as a Corvette. But for a short time the guy probably believed he'd ruled the world, tooling around in the 'Vette. "Thanks for detailing it."

"Ya best thank the gals at the beauty shop."

A bunch of hairdressers had washed his sports car?

"All them gals in short shorts and skimpy tops a scrubbin' 'n a rubbin'. Ain't never seen nothin' like it in all my born years."

Sullivan swallowed a laugh at Jo's eye rolling.

"We're going to take the car for a drive. Mind if I leave my truck here?" she asked.

"Suit yerself."

A quick search of his wallet landed a twenty. Sullivan held out the money. "For stowing the car."

"Use it fer gas." Amos fished the keys from his pocket, then walked off with a wave. The old fart's taxi service had probably netted more than twenty bucks.

After helping Jo into the 'Vette, he slid into the driver's seat. Before he started the car, she argued, "When are you going to learn that paying for favors is an insult?"

"Probably never." He grinned at the engine's soft hum.

"While you gas up, I'll buy us a picnic lunch from the café."

A picnic in the country with a beautiful woman—Sullivan was beginning to believe life in the *holler* had its rewards.

JO AND SULLIVAN sat on a soft blanket of grass and watched the waters of Periwinkle Creek float by. The mountain-fed stream flowed through several communities, and Jo had picked the location—twenty miles outside Finnegan's Stand—because huge gum trees lined the banks, providing shade and privacy from the road.

Curling her legs to the side, she tugged at the hem of her dress, wishing she'd worn pants to church. Sullivan's heated stare strayed to her bare feet, igniting tiny sparks inside her. "Hungry?" she asked.

His heavy-lidded gaze moved to her bodice and her pulse jumped a beat. "I meant food," she admonished, hiding her smile as she retrieved the sandwiches she'd purchased from the café. She couldn't ever remember Brian making her feel this giddy.

"Maybe in a little while." Sullivan lay back, crossed his arms behind his head and studied the tree branches above. "That was the first time I'd ever sat in a church and listened to a sermon."

The quiet admission tugged at Jo. "You didn't have an easy life, did you?"

"My mother never even tried to stop drinking. Not even for me."

His tone edged with pain, startled Jo. He'd always spoken matter-of-factly about his childhood in previous conversations. Now she heard his unspoken question: *Why wasn't I enough to make my mom seek help?* Without thinking, she brushed a strand of hair from his forehead, her fingers lingering against his temple.

"Once I became a teenager, I didn't care anymore. I managed to keep my distance from her by staying in school and working at fast-food joints nights and weekends."

"Did you have friends?"

"The kids at my job. But I didn't hang with them outside of work."

Such a lonely life. "Still, you did well for yourself."

He rolled to a sitting position. "You have a college degree. I don't."

"How did you end up working for a newspaper?"

"I applied at the newspaper and got hired to drive a delivery truck."

Living a sheltered life in the hollow, Jo had been reluctant to attend college after high school. If not for her grandfather's insistence that she must understand the outside world in order to appreciate her own heritage, she might not have applied. "How did you become a reporter?"

"Every day I read the paper front to back. I decided to try my hand at writing a story and I put together a short feature on a Vietnam vet who I'd gotten to know in one of the shelters my mother and I lived in for a while. I guess I had a knack for words. After a year of delivering papers, I was hired to do obituaries."

"Obituaries?" She laughed.

"Hey, it was a bump in pay."

Jo considered assuring him that his mother would have been proud of what he'd accomplished, but couldn't because she suspected the woman wouldn't have cared. "You went from obit writer to reporter, I'm impressed."

"Until now, I'd decided hard work was more important than a college diploma or who your parents were or weren't. But after all my years of struggling, I'm not sure."

"What do you mean?"

"Without a college degree or the influence of a family name, I doubt I'll ever climb higher than being an editor."

Sullivan and Jo had one thing in common; although they were from different worlds, they'd each experienced being looked down upon by others.

Before Jo could find the words to reassure him, he popped off the ground and strolled to the water's edge. With his back to her, he confessed, "All I ever wanted was to be *somebody*. A man others envied."

That he believed he wasn't worthy unless he achieved stardom made Jo leave her seat on the grass and go to him. His brown eyes glazed with pain humbled her. That he allowed her to witness his agony moved her to tears.

How could she admire a man who had little in common with her? She shoved the thought aside, wishing only to comfort him. At this moment, Sullivan wasn't a newspaper reporter, he was a man. A man she yearned very much to kiss. Rising on tiptoe, she feathered her mouth across his.

With her lips and soft sighs Jo showed Sullivan that she valued him as a person. That she found him worthy. Attractive. When she'd gone to him, she'd had no idea where she'd wanted the kiss to lead, but her racing pulse and thundering heart cried for more.

Sullivan must have sensed the yearning building inside her, because he wrapped his arms around her waist and brought her body to his. His hand clutched her hip, pressing her tighter to his arousal. Her fingers grasped his hair, urging him to deepen the kiss. She shivered at the first taste of his tongue. Sullivan's touch left a trail of heat unlike anything she'd ever experienced.

His hands mussed her hair, his fingers dragging across her scalp, cupping the back of her head. He moaned as their tongues danced. Time crept by as slow as the current near their feet. Breaths grew shorter…faster. Muscles ached and trembled…burned.

"Sweet heaven," he murmured after breaking the kiss.

"You're saying that because you went to church this morning."

He squeezed her bottom playfully, his hand lingering over the round swell, then sliding lower to dip beneath the hem of her dress, where he caressed the back of her thigh. He tilted her chin, their gazes connecting. No words had to be spoken.

I want you, Jo.

I want you, too, Sullivan.

Brown eyes narrowed. But…

What about tomorrow? Her life was on the mountain—Sullivan's over two thousand miles away. Even though he'd made himself at home among the clan, he would always be a flatlander. He might insist he understood and even sympathized with the clan's unique position in the world, but he would never be one of them.

Do we have to care about the future, Jo? Let this moment be enough for now.

Did she dare give herself permission to explore the crazy heat that had been developing between them since the moment she'd spotted Sullivan running from Jeb's hounds? Her mind sped forward in time and she envisioned herself a weary old woman, alone in her cabin with nothing more than memories for comfort. Sullivan's eyes promised a memory for all time—an afternoon delight with a big-city newspaper reporter beneath a gum tree on the banks of Periwinkle Creek.

"Too soon?" He tucked a strand of hair behind her ear, his finger lingering against her skin.

She lifted her mouth to his. "Too right."

Chapter Ten

Afternoon sun filtered through the limbs of the black gum tree, dotting the cushion of green grass along the creek bank with spots of white light. Jo wasn't worried a passerby might intrude on her and Sullivan's lovemaking—the road they'd driven along was not often used by the locals. But she was concerned about sharing their love nest with the insects. A swollen, itchy spider bite on the rear was hardly romantic. "You wouldn't happen to have a blanket stowed in the car, would you?"

He flashed a dimple. Amazing how the little dent in his cheek had the power to spin Jo's head.

"As a matter of fact…" He confiscated the keys from his pants pocket, pointed the fob at the car and activated the trunk release.

When Jo had first seen the red Corvette, she'd hated it on sight because it represented the outside world. Reminded her of Brian and the fancy sports car he'd driven when she'd dated him in college. But after today's ride, she'd changed her mind and decided the 'Vette was pure sex on wheels. She'd love to race the sport machine along the switchback roads in the hollow, the tires barely clinging to the edge of the mountain, but she doubted Sullivan would hand over the keys to his *baby*.

His love for the vehicle had been evident in his expression

as they'd cruised to the picnic spot. The corners of his mouth had curved and excitement had shone in his eyes. Watching the muscles in his thighs bunch when he shifted gears had been such a turn-on that she'd had to shove her fingers under her thighs to keep from reaching for his leg. *Soon I'll touch those thighs all I want.*

After Sullivan removed a royal-blue blanket from the trunk, he returned to her side. She helped spread the material across the ground, making sure the corners were straight.

The width of the cloth separating them might as well have been an ocean, so different were their worlds, their goals. Never had Jo faced a more worthy adversary than Sullivan. Yet the tenderness radiating from his expression insisted that once they lay down, their differences would evaporate like early-morning mountain fog. Even so, there was one problem… "I don't—"

"What?" Apprehension flickered across his handsome features.

Suppressing a smile at his worry that she'd changed her mind, Jo knelt in the center of the blanket. "I'm not on any birth control."

Eagerly he grasped for the wallet in his back pocket. "I always carry a condom with me."

Her heart winced. There had been no one since Brian. Sullivan would end a six-year dry spell. She wanted their lovemaking to be more than a one-afternoon stand. What she felt for him went deeper than sexual attraction. Thanks to Brian, she'd learned the difference between infatuation and genuine caring. The desire to know she *mattered* to Sullivan drove the question from her mouth. "Do you do this often?"

Too absorbed in studying the condom wrapper, he didn't answer her. A moment later, he swore. "The thing's expired."

Relief loosened the last tenuous hold she claimed over her

emotions. Free to welcome him, to embrace this moment, she assured him, "It will be fine."

Worry shadowed the hollows of his cheeks. He cared about the consequences, cared about her—more than she'd expected. More than she'd hoped for.

"You're positive, Jo?"

She lifted her arms in invitation.

Joining her on the blanket, close enough that his belt buckle gouged her hip, he reached out his callused fingers and stroked her cheek. "If anything happens—" his throat muscles rippled "—you'll tell me, won't you?"

"Yes." Sullivan wasn't Brian. He wouldn't walk away from her or their child. And no matter that their individual goals stood between them, Sullivan would accept and embrace their child's Appalachian heritage.

"I don't even know how old you are." When she smoothed her finger across Sullivan's lower lip, he nibbled the tip.

"Thirty-eight." Then he palmed her breasts and Jo's breath caught. With Sullivan, there were no niceties. No pre-lovemaking moves or tentative forays—only bold touches and strokes.

His thumb strummed a nipple, nurturing an ache that grew in intensity. "I'm ten years younger," she confessed.

"You seem—" his gaze moved from his hand to her face "—wiser than your years."

"I'll take that as a compliment." Yearning for more than the touch of his hand, she arched her back, silently begging.

Hands pulled the dress sleeves off her shoulders, exposing her white lace bra. A sound of satisfaction rumbled in his throat seconds before he latched on to her nipple. At the subtle tug of his mouth, she threaded her fingers through his hair, her nails digging into his scalp.

While he pleasured her breasts, he released the clasp of her bra. As soon as her flesh popped free of the confinement, he buried his face in her cleavage. "You smell so good," he mumbled, his lips tickling her skin. "Your scent drives me wild. It's always there, even in my dreams."

He dreams about me... Jo curled a leg around his thigh and thrust her aching center against his arousal. Her fingers fumbled with his shirt and he swept her hands aside, pulling the material over his head. She rubbed her nose across his chest muscles, inhaling his unique masculine scent and hint of lemon from the bath soap—a trace of Appalachian Mountain covered his skin.

While her mouth familiarized itself with the planes and dips of his chest, Sullivan worked her dress over her hips and down her legs. He flung the silky material aside. Her bra followed. Then he sought her mouth, his tongue mimicking the movement of his fingers between her thighs.

Jo's body quaked with little tremors. *Already?* At times, she felt as if her entire life had been spent fighting one cause or another. This was a battle she'd gladly concede. The wall she'd erected between her and Sullivan crumbled beneath his skillful caresses. She opened her eyes, the bright daylight adding to the eroticism of the moment—no darkness to hide their expressions. No covers to crawl beneath. Everything in plain sight.

Exposed. Vulnerable. Her feelings reflected in the dark pools of brown watching her. There were no pretty phrases between them. She didn't want words. When he shimmied down her body, his mouth trailing a wet path along her skin, she gifted him with a moan.

Then his lips caressed her damp panties right before he worked the material over her hips and down her legs. His knuckles grazed the hairs at the apex of her thighs. "Fire. The color of forging heat." He tilted his head, his eyes beseeching. "Burn for me, Jo. Burn." He buried his mouth between her thighs and she swooped through the valleys and soared above the peaks of Heather's Hollow.

Unsure how long her flight had lasted, Jo drifted back to earth and curled against Sullivan.

"I've wanted you since the moment you stormed into your grandfather's fishing cabin the morning after you'd abducted me." Sullivan's admission sighed across the top of her head.

Clinging to the tingling remnants of her orgasm, Jo purred, "Not before?"

Big hands stroked her back, curved around her hip and nestled her closer. "If I'd known what lay underneath that floppy felt hat and those baggy overalls, I would have wanted you even with your shotgun staring me in the face." He tilted her chin. "Johanna…Johanna. Your name is as beautiful as you are—softness over steel."

"Being compared to a piece of metal is hardly flattering." She nipped his chest.

"Steel is smooth," he insisted, running his hands over her neck and across her shoulders. "And sometimes hot to the touch." He dipped a finger inside her and she bucked at the quick caress. "Or cold." He licked her nipple, then blew until the nub hardened.

"Okay, it was a compliment." Smiling, she stretched like a lazy cat, raising her arms above her head. "Your turn."

Sullivan sprang from the blanket, stumbling as he toed off his shoes. He tugged his belt, then shucked his pants and tossed his socks over his shoulder. His eagerness fueled Jo's confidence in her femininity. He stood before her, face hidden in the shadows, his chest rising and falling. A trim waist connected to strong, sturdy thighs and… *Oh, my.*

Then he pounced. Skin to skin. Limbs entwined. Mouths fastened together. Urgency stole the air from her lungs as her body rushed into a fray of arousal and emotion. Her insides sizzled and churned as sensation found an opening of escape and clawed its way to the surface, where it exploded in a desperate burst of energy.

Shoving against Sullivan's chest, she rolled him to his back. Clasping his head between her hands, she drove her tongue into his mouth, searching for a connection that the outside world was powerless to break. Heart thundering against her rib cage, she struggled forward, unable to change direction, yet fearing what lay ahead. "Now," she breathed into his mouth. "Now, Sullivan."

She grasped his length, stroked once, twice, then stole the last of his resistance when she teased him with her mouth. He didn't protest when she rolled the condom on or when she guided him inside her. She moved hard and fast, focusing on her own desire and pleasure. This coupling was beyond her control...beyond her understanding. No rhythm. No finesses. Simply a wild ride.

Frustrated, she hung suspended over a precipice. Then Sullivan was there. With a hand between her thigh and his mouth on her breast, he cut the rope.

And she plunged to a glorious death.

When consciousness returned, the first sounds to filter into Jo's brain were the buzzy notes of the cerulean warbler from the tree branches above her head. Then she felt the stir of Sullivan's breath against her temple. Sprawled across his chest, she savored the weakening tingles and twinges from her dizzying climax. She refused to analyze the consequences of an experience she feared unique only to her and Sullivan. She savored. Reveled. Absorbed.

"You okay, Johanna?"

Johanna...a breathless caress escaping from his mouth.

"Yes." She kissed his sweaty neck, sampling his salty taste. She'd never experienced anything this sensual or seductive. The bumbling beneath the covers with Brian had been awkward, unexciting and painful because she'd been a virgin.

Basking in the warmth of Sullivan's embrace, she felt a movement, a stirring of a part his anatomy still connecting them. "Didn't you…" she asked, propping herself up on his chest.

He grinned.

Good grief! She'd been so caught up in her own pleasure she hadn't even realized Sullivan hadn't… "I'm sorry."

"No way are you apologizing for the most mind-blowing experience I've ever had with a woman." He peeled away the damp clump of hair sticking to her neck. "You were amazing."

The awe in his voice soothed her worry that she'd hogged the spotlight. "Well, then." She sampled his mouth. "I get to watch you." The words stalled in her throat, but she gazed into his eyes, begging him to prove that what they'd shared hadn't been a fluke. Hadn't been the result of her being celibate for too many years.

Sullivan got down to business. With hands and mouth, he rekindled the fire from the ashes of their previous lovemaking. He dragged her along the burning path, exhausting her emotionally and physically, until together they exploded toward a destiny outside their control.

LONG STRANDS of red hair stuck to Sullivan's naked chest and arms. His hands twitched with desire to spread Johanna's locks over his shoulders and snuggle beneath the softness. He'd never been with a woman who gave everything during lovemaking the way Jo had. Her bold, unhesitant responses and willingness to allow him a glimpse of the erotic, earthy woman inside her had inflated his ego to a dangerous level.

Hidden under the layers of her determined-to-save-the-clan armor lay a vulnerable woman. A woman who begged for independence, yet at the same time yearned for protection.

Damned if he didn't crave to be her protector. His chest tightened as he thought of Jo going through life alone, raising Katie by herself. Struggling to achieve her goal to keep the clan's solidarity intact. Part of him wanted to stand by her side and help shoulder those burdens. Share her successes. Rejoice in her victories. Cry with her when she failed—unusual for a man who put his own needs before others.

But another part wondered what was the matter with him. A few moments in Jo's arms and all of a sudden everything he'd worked for his entire life lost its importance? Lost its allure? What spell had she cast on him to create such a powerful urge to champion *her* cause and make *her* dreams—not his—come true?

Love. Had he fallen in love with Jo? Shoot, he wouldn't recognize the sentiment if it bit him in the ass. He'd never allowed himself to get serious with a woman in the past. Why would he cave in to Jo? *Because she makes you feel. She stirs you the way no other woman ever has. Stop,* his mind cried. He anticipated where the conversation was headed and he refused to go there.

You're afraid.

Sullivan blamed his inability to love on a crummy childhood and a mother who didn't know how to show affection. Or was that an excuse to protect his heart from more hurt? Is that why he'd ended all his relationships before the subject of marriage and family could even come up?

Marriage. Before making love to Jo, the word hadn't been in his vocabulary. His mind fast-forwarded through tomorrow, next week, next month, next year. Bleak. Empty. Boring. Long days at the newspaper, then retiring to an empty apartment— not even a pet to greet him at the door. What would it be like to return home each evening to Jo's smile and Katie's hug?

A tight feeling pinched his lungs as he imagined walking away from Jo, Katie and that goofy dog. He pressed Jo to him, memorizing the feel of her lush breasts against his chest. "How did you manage to work your way under my skin?" he whispered.

"That's me, all right—a tick."

Hand it to Jo to find humor in something as serious as heartache. He moved her head until their mouths connected. After a thorough kiss, he confessed, "I don't have any experience with long-term relationships. But right now, Red, I'm having a hell of a time picturing me leaving you."

Her blue gaze fastened to something over his shoulder. Had he said too much too soon? He'd witnessed her response to their lovemaking—too genuine to be faked. Maybe he should guard his feelings before he made promises he couldn't keep. He lost himself in another kiss, their tongues stroking, tangling, playing.

They surfaced for air and, Jo asked, "Why did you buy a Corvette?"

Surprised by the question, he offered a flippant response. "Because it's a babe magnet."

"You're lying." She swatted his shoulder playfully.

Would she think less of him if he told her the truth? "My mother could barely keep a roof over our heads when I was a kid." That was an understatement. "We didn't have many possessions and what belonged to us was previously owned." Jo's calloused hand moved over his chest and he imprisoned her fingers. "Stop. I can't concentrate when you touch me." She giggled, and he treasured the lighthearted sound—at odds with the normally serious woman. "I'd gone through life being a nobody, Jo. A boy who wore hand-me-down clothes and qualified for the free-lunch program in school. Kids mocked me. Claimed I was white trash. A loser." He hated discussing his childhood and questioned whether he'd ever be able to put the past behind him.

Dragging her toes up and down his calf, she murmured incoherent noises that made him believe the peace he sought might be found in her arms. "I'd decided when I grew up that I'd be a person others would envy." Saying the words made Sullivan sound shallow and immature. He buried his face in Jo's hair and breathed her in—part of him wishing he'd never continued this far with her, never mind chasing a legend he had little chance of catching. He managed to rein in his emotions, and with a parting kiss against her forehead, he slipped from her arms.

"We'd better dress before someone happens along." Keeping his eyes averted, he threw his clothes on, then walked to the creek bank and studied the slow-moving water.

The past few weeks he'd felt as if he'd fallen into a fairy tale. All these years he'd convinced himself he hadn't needed a family. That being alone in the world was better. Safer. That his job was enough to keep him happy. Content. That the Corvette was proof he'd become a person of importance. He was such a fool.

Family, not a car, was what Sullivan yearned for. An afternoon in a woman's arms—Jo's arms—had rudely awakened a desire he'd buried deep within himself—a family to claim his own. A home. A place to belong. A place where *he* mattered.

Her fleeting touch interrupted his musings. He winced at the worried expression on her face. "Everything's going to be okay," he reassured her, struggling to believe his own words.

"Sullivan—"

A finger against her swollen, pouty lips halted the apology. *Sorry* wasn't a word he wanted associated with their lovemaking. He sniffed, catching the faint scent of singed wood. "Do you smell smoke?"

Jo shielded her eyes from the sun and scanned the hills. "Oh, no."

Following her line of sight, he spotted the black cloud forming above the treetops. "Fire."

LOST IN THOUGHT as the Corvette raced toward the gristmill, Jo was a basket case. Making love with Sullivan had been an earth-shattering experience. One she'd cherish the rest of her life. Before she'd had the opportunity to soak in all the nuances associated with being intimate with Sullivan, he'd yanked her heartstrings when he'd presented a glimpse of his impoverished childhood. That he'd assumed a car would make others stand up and take notice of him brought tears to her eyes. She'd wished to reassure him that he mattered simply because he was a human being, but they'd been interrupted by the smell of smoke. Now she could add frayed nerves to her unstable state.

When they reached the gristmill, Amos lounged on the fender of Jo's truck. "Where's the fire?" she bellowed out the window before Sullivan put the car into Park.

"Kavenagh's barn." Amos tossed the truck keys to her.

"Anyone hurt?" she asked, ignoring how the old man's eyes perused her rumpled clothing and mussed hair.

"Ain't heard."

Sullivan rounded the hood of the 'Vette and handed off his keys to Amos—a game of musical keys. "I'll fetch the car later. Let's go, Jo." He hopped in the passenger side of the truck.

The engine sputtered and shook, then she gunned the gas, spewing dust into the air when the truck shot forward. Only through town did she ease up on the accelerator. As she navigated the winding roads into the hollow, Sullivan's fingernails dug into the seat cushion. Poor man probably feared she'd drive them off the mountainside. "Don't worry. I can handle this road with my eyes closed."

"Don't show off for me," he teased. At the bridge crossing Periwinkle Creek, he asked, "How long before the local fire department arrives?"

"What fire department?"

"Doesn't Finnegan's Stand have fire service?"

"The nearest station is two towns over. Thirty minutes by highway."

"Wouldn't someone in Finnegan's Stand phone in the emergency?"

"There's nothing they can do. The hollow doesn't have any water mains or pipes to hook up a hose. The sawmill owns a pump truck that can be filled with river water. I'm sure they've asked for the truck."

"What about forest fires?"

Jo wished she could believe that natural curiosity prompted Sullivan's questions, but she knew better. Her answers would find their way into his story. At least the information had come from her and not an outsider. "We had a decent-sized fire when I was a little girl. Burned over two thousand acres. The U.S. Forest Service took control. Brought in the National Guard and they used inmates from the Bell County Forestry Camp facility to contain the blaze."

"Were there any deaths?"

"No, thank goodness. But the sawmill lost over a thousand acres of trees. The mill never recovered. Laid off close to a hundred men and dropped to one shift."

"That's rough."

"Most of the men who'd lost their jobs relocated their families to the city to find work."

"How many men does the mill employ now?"

"Around sixty."

"The entire hollow is here," he commented as Jo maneuvered her truck between the vehicles alongside the drive leading to Kavenagh's property. She parked a hundred yards from the burning barn. Both she and Sullivan bolted into the fray.

Several men wielded the water hose from the pump truck, aiming at the structure's roof. A dark cloud hovered above the barn and acrid black smoke billowed from the doors. The women had begun a bucket brigade and passed well water to the men. "I'm going to go join the line," Jo shouted.

Bucket after bucket marked the passage of time. As soon as the pump truck left to refill its water tank, the barn roof collapsed, spitting ash and cinder everywhere. A half hour later, the walls caved in and Suzanne Kavenagh stopped struggling to pump well water. Arms aching, Jo hugged the older woman. No words were spoken. This was the price the clan paid for choosing to live in the hollow, secluded from major towns and cities. A price most would gladly pay over and over again.

Jo scanned the milling crowd for Sullivan. He stood with his back to her, covered in soot and grime, his gaze on the forge, which was visible in the rubble. When the debris cooled, neighbors would help Tom cart it away and sift through the remains, searching for salvageable tools or machines.

Tom approached, wearing a brave smile. "Sullivan saved my hammers, Suzanne. We'll rebuild."

Suzanne's eyes glistened with tears. "I reckon we will." She pressed her cheek to her husband's sooty chest.

The pain on Tom's face was more than Jo could stand. She left the couple to grieve in private and went to Sullivan. "Are you all right?" He didn't answer, his concentration on the ruined structure. Fatigue lined his dirty, sweaty face and a nasty scrape marred his forearm. "You're hurt."

"A scratch. I'll clean it later."

Refusing to allow her heart advantage over her anger, she scolded, "You shouldn't have run into the burning barn." She remembered how her heart had lodged in her throat when she'd caught sight of Sullivan charging through the smoke and flames. She'd sprinted after him, only to skid to a halt when he'd stumbled from the structure, arms loaded with heavy equipment.

"I knew where the hammers were."

She threw herself at Sullivan, hugging the life out of him.

He'd risked everything for a bunch of stupid hammers and put himself in danger for a man he hardly knew.

He cares, Jo. But if you acknowledge that, then you'll have to admit you care. Maybe more than care. Maybe love. As if he were a piece of smoldering wood scorching her hands, she dropped her arms from around him.

"Mooreland done good, Jo. City slicker's turned into a country boy." Kavenagh pounded Sullivan's shoulder.

Wincing, Sullivan clamped his lips together to keep from groaning. He'd almost escaped unscathed from the burning barn, when a piece of roof had fallen and clunked him on the back seconds before he'd reached the door.

Despite the pain, he hadn't felt this good, this satisfied, this important in a long time—if ever. He'd never been involved in a situation where he'd been needed in the way Kavenagh and the others had depended on his help today. No one had minded who he was, where he'd hailed from or that he drove a red Corvette. They'd welcomed him into the group simply because he was a man willing to help.

Sullivan was under no illusion that his heroic efforts had magically secured him membership in the clan, but for an instant he'd mattered.

Sullivan Mooreland belonged somewhere—here in Heather's Hollow.

Chapter Eleven

"Was it a big fire, Mr. Sully?" Katie asked, plunking down on the porch step next to Sullivan.

Eavesdropping, Jo hovered out of sight behind the screen door. By the time she'd collected her daughter from the pastor's home earlier in the evening, word of the reporter's heroics had spread through the hollow. She'd spent the past two hours on the phone answering questions.

Who's this stranger livin' in the hollow?

He got kin here?

A reporter, you say? What sort of shenanigans is he pullin'?

Why's he snoopin' 'round our backyard?

Don't trust no flatlander. He ought to mosey along 'afore he meets up with a heap o' trouble.

"Yeah, Katie bug," Sullivan explained, "the fire was big and hot."

Katie bug. Sullivan had taken to using the nickname several days ago and the endearment caused Jo heartache. The two looked so right together, sitting side by side. A stranger would be hard-pressed to guess Sullivan wasn't Katie's real father.

Her daughter's easy acceptance of Sullivan was the cause of Jo's restless nights. She was no longer certain she wished Katie to grow up being distrustful of anyone outside the clan.

Tired of the rumors, the novels and movies that sensationalized Appalachian culture, Jo wouldn't succeed in her game if outsiders continued to be ignorant of the Appalachian culture. Knowledge, tolerance and respect from both sides were essential for success. She anticipated that in order to achieve a broader, more sweeping understanding of the clan's heritage, their *story* would have to be told in person—not written in a newspaper that was read one day and thrown out with the trash the next.

The Scotch-Irish clan claimed a rich history of storytelling. Tales passed from generation to generation orally. Someone had to recount the story of Heather's Hollow. Yet the prospect of leaving her home, of facing crowds of intolerance, bigotry and prejudice freaked her out.

"Did you get an owie in the fire?" Katie rested her tiny fingers on his bandaged arm.

"Yes, but your mom patched me up." He put away the notepad he'd been scribbling on and gave his full attention to Katie.

"Mama's a good boo-boo fixer."

"Your mama has a lot of talents, Katie bug, the least of which is sticking a Band-Aid on a scratch."

"What kind of talents?"

"Well, for one, she's real pretty, don't you think?"

Katie's head bobbed, her curls tumbling over her shoulder.

"And she makes a mean sawmill gravy."

"And a mean chocolate cake," Katie added with a giggle.

Land sakes, eavesdropping was good for Jo's ego.

"And your mama's real smart. She went off to college and learned how to be a teacher."

"I'm gonna be a teacher when I grow up."

"Teachers are important people."

"Is Mama an important people?"

"One day Johanna Macpherson is going to be famous." He leaned closer. "But she doesn't know it yet."

"What's she gonna do?"

"Teach people all over the world about Heather's Hollow."

"The whole world can't fit inside Mama's itty-bitty school."

"Not the school in the hollow. A big university. And one day your mama's going to be on television."

Katie's mouth dropped open right along with Jo's. Why was Sullivan filling her daughter's head with such nonsense?

Stepping onto the porch, she announced, "Time for bed, honey."

"Mama." Katie popped off the step. "Mr. Sully says you're gonna be important."

"He does, does he?"

"Can I be important, too?"

"Of course, sweetie." Her daughter's generation might very well be the first to bridge the intolerance gap.

"'Night, Mr. Sully."

"Sweet dreams, Katie bug." As soon as the door closed, Sullivan's gaze landed on Jo. Awareness crackled between them like heat lightning. "Will you sit with me after tucking her into bed?" His eyes asked, *are you up for more than talking?*

Given the choice, she'd rather not talk. Less than twenty minutes later, she had Katie snuggled under the covers, a story read and three kisses blown from the doorway. Once downstairs, she detoured into the kitchen, grabbed two cans of Dr Pepper from the fridge and joined Sullivan on the porch.

"What's this?" His face lit up at the sight of the pop.

"For being a hero today." She sat next to him on the step.

"If I drink this, I'll want more and more and more."

"Don't worry. I bought a twelve-pack."

"When?" he wheezed after guzzling half the can.

"After retrieving Katie from Fiona's, I stopped in Finnegan's Stand."

"Man, that tasted great. Thanks."

"You're welcome." Mountain noise filled the stretch of silence. Birds. Wind. Tree branches rustling. Twigs snapping. Good sounds. Comforting sounds. Sounds of *home*.

Sullivan's eyes skimmed over her face before perusing the ingredients on the Dr Pepper can. "You probably want to talk about what happened today."

"No, I'm tired of discussing the fire."

"I meant *before* the fire." Brown eyes measured. Waited.

"There are a lot of notions clogging my head, but I've yet to make sense of them."

"Does what we shared this afternoon have to make sense?" He rested his hand on her knee, applying the right amount of pressure to interfere with clear thinking. "Can't we let it be for now?"

She sympathized with his point of view. If they overanalyzed what had transpired under the shade of the black gum tree, they'd chance missing out on more of the same thing. But Jo couldn't afford not to consider the risks of deepening her relationship with Sullivan. Making love with him had shaken her control. He'd snagged a piece of her heart with his touches and kisses and she hesitated to allow him a bigger chunk.

"I'm leaning toward letting it be, Sullivan, but I do have a question."

Masculine fingers stroked the inside of her knee, further messing with her concentration. He tilted his head and murmured in her ear, "Ask me anything." Then he nipped the sensitive flesh between her neck and shoulder.

"What exactly is it that you don't want us to let be?"

"*It* can be anything we want." He had an annoying habit of studying her mouth while she spoke.

"*It* can be a kiss." He moved his lips over hers—a fleeting caress.

"*Or it* can be…" He whisked aside her long hair and swirled his tongue inside her ear, his warm breath producing an explosion of goose pimples across her skin.

"Or…" He cupped her breast and licked her lower lip.

"Or…" His hand slid between the apex of her thighs and he stroked her through the denim.

"Or…"

Oh, *my*. She got the picture. She clasped his face between her hands. "I'm not going to lie to you, Sullivan. I want to make love with you until there isn't an ounce of desire left in my body and then I want to make love all over again." She sucked in a deep breath. "But—"

He cut her off. "Scared?"

She shook her head. "Worried."

"About what?" He tucked her against his side and patted her head as if she were a child requiring comfort.

"Concerned you'll change my life in a way I won't be able to fix after you leave."

"Nothing stays the same forever, Jo."

NOTHING STAYS the same…nothing stays the same…

Jo stood in front of the kitchen window, keeping an eye on Katie while she played in the tree house. Almost a week had passed since the barn fire, and Sullivan's words still lingered in the back of her mind.

Until the reporter had landed in the hollow, Jo had been in charge of her own destiny. Sullivan didn't realize he held the power to flip her world upside down, and she feared that once he figured it out, she'd be incapable of preventing him from making the first move.

Deep in her heart she believed he'd never hurt her—not intentionally. He'd told her often the past week that he admired what she was doing for the clan, and insisted that he'd tell the true story when he wrote his article for the paper. "Trust me, Jo," he'd said. She wanted to…desperately wanted to.

"What do mountain folk do for entertainment on Friday nights?" Sullivan asked, interrupting her reverie at the kitchen sink. He paused at her side and twisted a strand of her hair around his finger. The heat in his gaze told her he didn't expect an answer to his question.

Inch by inch, he closed the gap between their mouths, but instead of kissing her, he dipped his head and touched his lips to the curve of her neck. She arched, begging without words for a real kiss. He obliged, plunging his tongue inside her mouth. He tasted of peppermint and… She lost her train of thought when his arousal bumped her stomach. "Please tell me your people make out on Friday nights," he murmured in her ear, then sucked the lobe.

How she wished she could spend the night in his arms on the couch. Make popcorn and watch an old movie together, but she had other plans—plans that couldn't be changed.

"Will you do me a favor?" she asked in a hushed voice.

His hand curved over her buttocks. "Anything."

"Babysit Katie tonight?"

"Why? Have a hot date?" His fingers tensed against her flesh.

His attempt at humor deserved a smile. "I have to work at the still. Usually Granny stays at the house while I'm gone, but since you're here…"

"Let me tag along." He wiggled his eyebrows suggestively.

"That's exactly why you shouldn't. Nothing would get done." This time she initiated the kiss…thrust her tongue inside his mouth…

"You're not sneaking off to meet with Lightning Jack, are you?"

He'd voiced the question in jest, but Jo caught the flicker of uncertainty in his eyes before he blinked. "I promise I'm not meeting Lightning Jack." That was the truth. The other part about working the still…was a lie. But she didn't dare confide in him that she had to make a delivery tonight—across the county line almost two hours away.

"When will you return?"

"Before daybreak." When he cupped her cheek, she nuzzled the center of his palm, where the faint scent of smoke still clung to his skin.

"If you're not in the house when the sun rises, Katie and I are coming after you. That's my promise."

If she wasn't careful, Jo could become accustomed to his caring. "Deal."

As was his habit before he kissed her, he slid his fingers into her hair and tilted her head a fraction. Not a chaste goodbye kiss, but a please-return-home-safe kiss. Sweet, slow, thorough. "I'll be waiting for you."

After retrieving the keys and cell phone, she headed for the truck. The phone wouldn't do much good if she ran into trouble, but, along with the shotgun under the front seat, it gave her peace of mind.

As she drove off, Sullivan waved from the porch, which he still hadn't moved from. This was one night she wished the truck's radio wasn't busted—music would have distracted her from thoughts of Sullivan and his blow-her-mind kisses.

By the time Jo arrived at the still, filled the earthenware jugs with heather whiskey and stowed them in the truck bed, a cold chill hung over her shoulders. She stretched her aching back muscles and listened to what the mountains had to say.

From a young age she'd been taught to respect nature. Rusting leaves often warned of intruders; eerie silences foreshadowed deeper trouble. Tonight the hills remained benignly quiet and Jo shook off her apprehension.

She loved the mountains that surrounded the hollow, but

once in a while she grew weary of the folklore deeply ingrained in her heritage. Often she believed the clan's suspicious nature was more of a curse than a self-defense mechanism protecting them from the outside world.

After extinguishing the lanterns, she hopped into the truck and maneuvered onto a dirt path only she and the elders knew existed. Running east to west, the footpath clung to the side of the mountain. Her grandfather's father and the men of his generation had created the route used to transport moonshine to various drop-off points. Over the years as bootlegging had decreased, alternative routes that had forked off the main artery became impassable with new forest growth.

Her grandfather had warned Jo against stopping on the road—she'd assumed because there was little more than a foot of earth between the truck and edge of the mountain. She shuddered when she imagined stepping out of the vehicle and free-falling to her death two thousand feet below. But tonight, walled in on both sides by trees and bushes that jumped out and scraped the truck as she crawled through the black tunnel, Jo considered that her grandfather's warning might have been for an entirely different reason.

Letting up on the accelerator, she steered the truck around a tight curve. As soon as she straightened the wheel, she slammed on the brakes. Ten feet in front of the bumper a tree lay across the road. Her gaze cut to the door locks. Assured they were down, she scanned the area illuminated by the high beams of the headlights. Nothing.

The tree trunk hadn't been there a month ago when she'd driven the route. She couldn't recall the date of the last storm that had blown through the hollow. *What if the tree had been cut down?* She gripped the wheel tighter and peered through the windshield. The tree roots were buried in the underbrush making it impossible to tell. Damn.

Skin prickling, Jo checked the rearview mirror. Nothing but pitch-blackness behind her. Driving back to the hollow in Reverse was out of the question. The tree was too large in diameter to plow over it and possibly damage the undercarriage of the truck. This left one option, move the tree off the road.

With an exasperated sigh, she rested her forehead on the steering wheel and closed her eyes. After several deep breaths, she convinced herself that this was no big deal. She'd roll the log to the side of the path and continue on. Confidence restored, she lifted her head…and her heart slammed against the wall of her chest. The breath in her lungs froze and her fingers strangled the steering wheel until the skin over her knuckles threatened to split.

Man or apparition?

Wearing a dark duster and hat, the man had a grizzled gray beard that hung to his belly. He looked gaunt and hardly a threat—save for the shotgun in his hand. Sweat broke out across her brow as she awaited his next move.

Slow and steadily, as if he had all night to toy with her, he raised his head and stared at her through the windshield. Even from this distance she saw his eyes were the color of ice water. Clear. Blue. Cold. He stepped over the log and moved toward the truck. Jo retrieved the rifle from under the seat.

The man never broke eye contact with her, and his bottomless stare sent shivers of fear through her. When he paused by the front bumper, her finger twitched against the trigger. She held her breath, waiting for his next move. Seconds ticked by, then he swept past the side of the truck, his coat swishing the driver's door as he vanished into the dark.

First Sullivan wanting to do a story on Lightning Jack and now this stranger popping up out of nowhere. Definite signs that Jo needed to find an alternate method to earn money for her school.

Maybe he'll slip off the side of the road. She chastised herself for the uncharitable thought. She didn't have to wait long to discover the stranger's intentions. Clanking pottery jugs revealed that he was stealing her liquor.

Not that she was about to stop him. Katie's face flashed before her eyes. Jo was breaking the law and risking her life for what—a few extra dollars to fund her school? She shook her head. Who ever said teachers were smart? If she made it through this little adventure tonight, she planned to do some serious thinking about her finances.

The stranger passed by her window again. He carried three jugs, which he placed on the road, then he rolled the tree trunk off to the side.

Anger burned her gut that this stranger demanded she pay a toll to use a route her family had forged and maintained for generations. Once he'd retrieved the whiskey jugs, he vanished into the woods.

Be grateful all he wanted was a little moonshine. With one hand on the wheel and her finger curled around the trigger of the shotgun, she drove on. Ten miles clicked off the odometer before she relaxed enough to drop her weapon to the floor.

How had the man known she'd be making a delivery tonight? Had he hidden in the underbrush and spied on her the other times she'd passed through the area…taking note of the time and day?

The mountains were full of secrets. Maybe this man was one of them. Where were his people? Or didn't he belong to a clan? Was he an escaped convict hiding from the law? A war veteran unable to assimilate back into society?

Not until Jo hit the open field of the Payton farm did the tightness in her chest ease. She guided the truck toward the lit barn—a beacon of safety. She drove inside and Earl Payton shut the barn doors behind her.

In his late fifties and as round as a pumpkin, Earl was

fourth-generation moonshine distributor—when he wasn't being a farmer. Earl had been buying moonshine from Lightning Jack for years, and his daddy before him. "Yer face is all white like ya seen a ghost, Jo."

She considered confiding in Earl about the tree incident, but couldn't take the chance men might discover the secret road while searching for the trespasser. Besides, the stranger had done her no harm and she doubted they'd cross paths again. "Are Harriet and the boys well?"

"Family's fine."

Earl's two boys attended college in Louisville and his wife worked at a gas station in Clearwater, thirty miles down the highway. The income Earl earned from selling Jo's moonshine paid for his kids' education. People came from miles away to buy whiskey from Earl because he charged a fair price and never cheated customers by watering down the product. If Earl wondered who made the moonshine or why Jo, an educated schoolteacher made the deliveries, he didn't ask. As long as he got his liquor, he didn't care.

Fifteen minutes later they'd unloaded the jugs and reloaded the empty containers customers had brought back to the barn.

"I'm thinkin' yer short three jugs." He scratched his head.

"A few cracked during cleaning."

"Don't understand why ya gotta boil 'em in hot water. Menfolk ain't never complained of gettin' sick from drinkin' out of the jugs."

Maybe it was a woman thing, but she refused to refill an unwashed jug with moonshine and ruin the flavor. Tomorrow she'd begin the tedious task of sanitizing the earthenware inside and out to rid the jugs of tobacco juice and other unmentionables. Once in a great while she'd find treasure in a jug such as a soggy dollar bill or a woman's wedding band. Mostly she found spit and pee.

Earl handed her a wad of cash from a canning jar hidden beneath a bushel basket in the corner. She slid the money into her jeans pocket uncounted. "See you next month."

"Hey, Jo," he called as she got in the truck. "Roswell clan is havin' a jamboree July Fourth. Got kin comin' from the Carolinas. They're askin' fer a double order."

"I'll let Lightning Jack know," she lied. With a wave, Jo drove from the barn and crossed the field to the trail. As much as she hated the idea of another encounter with the stranger, she didn't dare risk taking the county road to the hollow. If she got pulled over by a deputy and he spotted the empty jugs in the truck bed, he'd assume she'd been delivering moonshine.

With a deep breath she headed into the belly of the mountain. Several miles later she checked the door locks and slowed the truck as she approached the spot where her liquor had been hijacked. As the truck crawled along, she scanned the sides of the road, searching for the fallen tree. Where was it? She stared hard at the woods but saw no evidence of a downed tree. *Darn it.* The mountain man had been real. She'd heard his footsteps. Heard the rustle of his clothing. Besides, what could be more real than three jugs of missing moonshine?

Let the mountain have its secret. She didn't want to think about the assailant anymore. By the time she drove into the front yard of the cabin, daylight flirted with the night sky and Sullivan stood on the other side of the screen door, hair mussed, eyes swollen with sleep.

She climbed the porch steps, wishing she could curl up with him on the sofa and sleep for ten hours. "Hi."

Without a word, he opened the door and hugged her. She breathed in his scent, sleepy male and faded bath soap. "I missed you," she murmured against his neck, too exhausted to care what he made of the declaration. How could she find the strength to let this man walk out of her life?

"The couch isn't as comfortable without you to share it with." He nuzzled her temple, while his hands rubbed her back, down her hips and cupped her fanny.

She nestled closer, savoring the knowledge that she aroused him. She lifted her head for his kiss and he didn't disappoint. Slow, thorough, he made love to her mouth. Nibbles, bold strokes and sweet pecks. By the time he broke the kiss, she was trembling.

"As much as I want to make love to you right now, Katie will be up soon." The regret in his voice soothed Jo's ego. "Why don't you relax in the tub and I'll bring you a cup of coffee," he suggested.

Good idea. A hot bath would relieve her tense muscles and aching back. Ten minutes later, Sullivan knocked on the door. "It's open."

The aroma of coffee preceded him into the room. He handed her a mug.

Sliding beneath the mounds of bath foam, she slurped. "Mmm, thanks."

"Here." He rolled a towel and shoved it behind her neck, then sat on the floor and leaned against the tub. "Everything go okay tonight?"

"Yep." She crossed her fingers and toes, hoping he'd let the subject drop. *Fat chance.*

"I've been pondering, Jo."

"That's not good." She hid a smile behind the mug. Did the man ever remove his reporter hat? A warm flush—not caused by the hot water—seeped through her body as she recalled one activity in which he'd ditched his interrogation tactics; making love.

Maybe she could fluster him again. After setting her mug on the window ledge, she threaded her fingers into Sullivan's hair, stopping him in midsentence. She loved his golden locks.

Soft and thick. Actually, she loved a lot of things about Sullivan. The dimple in his cheek. How his eyes turned dreamy, like now. The endearing way he placed his hand against her lower back when he motioned her to lead the way into a room. The caring tone in his voice when he spoke to Katie.

"What are you doing?" he growled, getting onto his knees and facing her.

"Touching you." When he grinned, she wiggled the tip of her finger against the tiny pit in his cheek.

"Why?" he asked.

"Because you're touchable."

"Katie will be awake soon." That Sullivan always kept her daughter in mind tweaked Jo's heart. If they had come from the same worlds, she wouldn't hesitate to sweep the man off his feet.

"Don't get me wrong," he continued, ignoring how she fiddled with the buttons on his shirt. "I admire your goal to teach the children to honor and respect their heritage. But I believe there's a bigger, more important issue at stake."

And it was that issue that separated them. "Go on," she encouraged him, deciding he wouldn't cease rambling until he'd made his point. She doubted Sullivan had ever instigated a conversation about inconsequential topics or indulged in chats that could be carried on even if the mind wandered.

"It's not only the clan's heritage at stake, Jo, but the whole Appalachian lifestyle."

Good grief. She inched higher in the tub until the tops of her breasts peeked above the water line. Sullivan's attention shifted to her breasts, and whatever else he'd proposed to say went unsaid. Pitying the poor man, she asked, "What's your point?"

"In order to preserve the clan's way of life and other Appalachian traditions and customs, the outside world needs to understand the culture. Once others accept you, the clan's children will be more apt to embrace their heritage."

She agreed with Sullivan, but argued, "Publicity goes against our desire for privacy. So does sharing our lives with the world."

"The clan doesn't have to be in the spotlight. One person, Jo. *You* take their story to the world. Before it's too late. Before the hollow and other places similar to it disappear for good."

That Sullivan had arrived at the same conclusion as her made it impossible for her to ignore the issue any longer. The teacher in her understood that ignorance bred intolerance. The only way to fight ignorance was with knowledge.

She remembered the pain, the embarrassment, the hurt of being ridiculed in college when Brian had used her. Was she willing to put herself in such a vulnerable position a second time? Could she afford not to?

She was so lost in thought that Sullivan startled her when he grabbed a washcloth. "I'll scrub your back." After he removed the coffee mug from her hand, she leaned forward and rested her chin on her bent knees.

The silky glide of the soapy rag elicited a groan of pleasure from her. "I'm making a trip into town to stock up on a few supplies," he whispered in her ear.

Supplies, meaning…condoms. She considered protesting. Insisting they were crazy to pursue a relationship. But then he moved the rag around to her breast.

The protest fizzled in her throat.

Chapter Twelve

"What's a barn raisin' without moonshine?" Jeb Riley drank from the tin cup Jo handed him. He puckered his face and spit. "What in tarnation?"

"Lemonade." Jo laughed. "You're too old to be drinking on the job. Once you finish for the day there will be plenty of whiskey to wet your whistle," she promised.

"Beauregard sure has taken a likin' to yer fella."

Her *fella* sat on the ground, attempting to keep his lunch out of the jaws of six drooling hounds. "I'm not claiming the man," Jo argued. Fighting a smile, she recalled the day she'd spotted Sullivan running for dear life from Jeb's animals. The flatlander had come a long way in a short time. She hadn't balked at inviting him to the barn raising today—a testament of how well he'd assimilated into her life.

When they'd arrived earlier that morning, her neighbors had greeted Sullivan with broad smiles and hearty handshakes, as if he were a fellow Scotsman.

It hadn't taken long before the men discovered Sullivan's enthusiasm wasn't supported by knowledge or skill. After he dropped a can of screws from the rafters and then tumbled off a scaffold, the group unanimously voted the flatlander gofer for the day.

The job of gofer in a barn raising was reserved for teenagers or young boys, but there weren't many adolescents left in the hollow willing to do it. Annie's boys would have helped, but today the twins had been instructed to watch over the younger children playing in the woods behind the Kavenagh cabin.

"He's a hard worker," Jeb complimented him. "Considerin' he's a city slicker."

If Sullivan minded the demotion, he didn't let on. While the West Coast reporter ran helter-skelter, fetching and carrying, Jo assisted the women with the cooking. Two weeks had passed since the blacksmith shop had caught fire. Neighbors had pitched in and helped Tom clear the debris. Tools had been salvaged, cleaned and repaired. The sawmill had generously donated a load of slightly flawed precut wood to build a new barn. Tom had inspected the planks and, aside from minor warping, decided they would do.

"Your hounds are slobbering all over Sullivan because he's feeding them scraps from his plate," Jo said.

"More 'n that, missy." Jeb nodded to the bean pot on the table. She ladled a second scoop onto his plate. "My hounds is good at judgin' folks. They trust the flatlander."

Trust—confounding word. "The dogs think anyone with food is good enough for them." She smiled when Beauregard rested his rump on Sullivan's thigh.

Jeb's dogs meant the world to him. His deceased wife had argued that her husband loved his dogs more than her. Ella had died of pneumonia five years earlier, and Jeb had adjusted to her loss better than anyone had expected. He was whistlin' Dixie now that he could bring his flea-ridden hounds inside the house.

The clan elders had worried about Jeb's ability to fend for himself—he'd never cooked a meal in all his eighty-odd years. It seemed the old coot didn't care if he had to eat beans and franks from a can every day. Granny invited Jeb to join her for a meal when the holidays rolled around, and that was all the socializing the widower cared for. He spent his days and weeks roaming the woods with his pack. Jo reckoned the mutts didn't mind that their master hadn't bathed or washed his clothes in months.

Once a year a group of women from the church marched over to Jeb's house and evicted him for the day. They scrubbed the walls and floor, bleached his bed linens, washed his clothes, dragged his mattress outside and beat it to within an inch of its life, and then Jo sprayed a store-bought pesticide in and around the cabin to kill the ticks and fleas.

Jeb groused over the invasion, but Jo believed he adored the attention. With a stern scowl she'd hand him a new pair of store-bought pants, a shirt, long johns and socks along with a bottle of flea shampoo. After five years, he knew the drill—he had to bathe himself and the dogs before he'd be allowed back inside the cabin.

Noticing the old man had cleaned his plate a second time, Jo informed him, "Suzanne has pies cooling on the kitchen table in the house."

Eyes sparkling, Jeb answered, "Sounds mighty fine." With a wink, he meandered across the yard and up the porch steps. He knocked first, then pressed his face against the door and sniffed. Jo heard Granny yell at him to stop poking in the screen. A moment later the door opened and Granny's gnarled fingers thrust a serving of apple pie at Jeb. He thanked her, then helped himself to a rocking chair, not the least bit offended he hadn't been invited inside.

"I admit it. Your man isn't a typical flatlander."

"Quit sneaking up on people," Jo accused when Annie popped out of nowhere. "And he's *not* my man." At least, not for long.

"Okay, then why have you been staring cow-eyed at the reporter all afternoon?"

"Since when is a covert glance considered a cow-eyed ogle?" She shouldn't...hated to ask...but darn, she had to know. "Are folks talking?"

"Wasn't that long ago you returned from college with a broken heart and a baby on the way. The clan doesn't forget when one of its own has been wronged."

"Sullivan's different." As soon as the words escaped, Jo ached to snatch them back.

"Maybe," Annie allowed.

The clan's opinion of Sullivan mattered. The clan was her family and she yearned for its approval. Dead or not, her grandfather meant the world to her and she didn't intend for her actions or choices to reflect badly on him. As a future candidate for the position of clan elder, she was held to a higher level of scrutiny than others. Hoping to steer the conversation in a different direction, Jo said, "I expected Sean to show up for the barn raising."

Annie studied the ground.

"Everything still not okay between you two?" Jo had no experience with marriage. Over the past twelve years she'd often wished she'd had more than a shoulder to offer her friend to lean on.

"When Sean comes home, all we do is argue. The mine has changed him. He's not the same man I dropped out of high school to marry."

Or Annie wasn't the same woman. Jo was tempted to remind Annie that she'd been the one to demand her husband seek a better-paying job and give up his position at the sawmill. "Has Sean considered asking for his old job back at the mill?"

"His former supervisor, Patrick Kirkpatrick, wants him back in a bad way. The man stopped by the cabin and offered Sean a raise if he'd return."

"That's good."

"No, it's not, Jo." Hands propped on her hips, she snapped, "Even with the raise, Sean wouldn't earn as much as he does mining. I want the boys to go to college and make something of themselves."

There was more at the heart of Annie's insistence that her husband earn a bigger paycheck than a simple wish to educate her sons, but Jo had no intention of prying.

"Don't understand why you returned home to the hollow after earning a teaching degree. You could have made more money in the city, instructing wealthy kids."

Not after her experience with filthy-rich Brian. That wasn't the life she wished for her or Katie. "Heather's Hollow is my home, Annie. This is where I belong."

"Yeah, well, I want a new washing machine."

Washing machine? What was that all about? Jo wondered as her friend headed for the well pump, where the twins were creating a ruckus.

Switching her attention from the commotion at the well to Sullivan, Jo realized they'd barely spoken to each other since they'd arrived at Tom's six hours ago. "Keep eyeballin' that man—" Granny rammed her bony elbow in Jo's side "—and weddin' rumors is gonna fly."

Good Lord, she should hole up somewhere out of sight until the men finished for the day. "There isn't going to be a wedding, Granny," Jo insisted. *No wedding,* despite Sullivan giving Jo the honeymoon she'd always dreamed of this past week. There had been a few changes of late—Sullivan now slept on the couch at night.

If Katie had noticed Sullivan's new sleeping quarters, she never commented. Jo remained upstairs with her daughter until the wee morning hours, then she'd sneak downstairs. Morphing into horny teenagers, she and Sullivan made love on the sofa, the kitchen counter, the back porch, the front porch and even in the truck bed under the stars. They'd almost exhausted the economy-sized box of condoms he'd purchased.

To Jo's way of thinking, life was perfect—accept for the fact that each time they made love she lost a bit of her heart to Sullivan. Neither of them had said the words *I love you.* Although her heart yearned to hear that declaration, she consoled herself with the knowledge that he cared deeply for her. Caring was enough. She ached inside when she envisioned the day he'd drive his flashy red Corvette down the road. She'd contemplated a long-distance relationship, but decided that wouldn't be fair to Katie. Her daughter deserved better than a part-time father. And Jo yearned for more than a long-distance, no-commitment affair.

"He say when he's leavin'?" Granny asked.

"No." This past week, she and Sullivan had struck an unspoken truce. Neither had brought up the subject of his feature story. Twice he'd gone into Finnegan's Stand to report to his boss, but he'd never discussed those conversations. And she hadn't asked.

"Appears ya gone and fell in love with the man. Ask him to stay."

"He's not one of us, Granny."

The elder frowned, the wrinkles around her mouth deepening until they swallowed her lips. "'Pears like one of us from where I'm standin'."

Lunch ended and the men brought their plates to the table by the porch. Sullivan patted the heads of Jeb's hounds before joining the crew. He hadn't spoken about his childhood since the afternoon they'd made love along the riverbank, but the way he responded to Jeb's dogs made her believe he'd always wished for a pet. Her throat tightened when she realized a dog would have given him more love than his mother had.

"He does seem to be having a good time," Jo conceded. Once, she'd caught Sullivan's unguarded expression, and the excitement on his face assured her he considered the barn raising a high-flying adventure. The clan men had participated in plenty of raisings during their lives and viewed the event as a necessity and nothing more.

Most days in the hollow were uneventful and packed with mundane chores and responsibilities. And Sullivan had never spent a winter in these mountains. Blustery winds swept down the hillsides, while snow and ice storms imprisoned them in their homes for days on end. And that was just the winter. Spring brought gullywashers and occasional tornados. "Sullivan's a reporter, Granny. We've no use for newspapers in the hollow."

"Reckon the man could find somethin' worth doin' if he put his mind to it." Granny drifted off to assist in the lunch cleanup.

Jo closed her eyes against the flicker of hope ignited by the old woman's words. Admittedly she'd fantasized about a life with Sullivan. After witnessing how easily he'd assimilated into the group today, Jo was tempted to imagine they had a chance at their own happy-ever-after.

The Appalachian Mountains were a world away from the hustle and bustle of Seattle. After a while, would the dense forests suffocate him? Would he miss dining in fancy restaurants and conversing with coworkers who were well informed about global events and world issues? The clansmen were more concerned about rainfall levels than they were about Congress voting itself another pay raise. How would Sullivan adjust to the knowledge that many of his neighbors didn't fret over outside controversies?

"Mama." Katie tugged Jo's pant leg. "Can I climb a tree with Bobby and Tommy?"

"What tree?" Jo licked her finger, then wiped a dirt smudge from her daughter's cheek.

"Um…" She shrugged. "One in the woods?"

There were hundreds of trees on Kavenagh's property. "No, honey. You might fall and knock yourself silly." She scanned the area for a sign of the twins. "Bobby and Tommy better not climb any trees, either." Annie didn't need the aggravation of her sons breaking more bones.

"Promise I won't fall," her daughter begged.

"No. I mean it, Katie."

Her daughter stuck out her lower lip and pouted.

"Mrs. Seamus could use your help collecting dirty dishes. Now, off with you." Jo waited to see that her daughter obeyed, then entered the Kavenagh cabin. With Suzanne's crippled hands, the simple task of washing dishes was often more than she could handle. Maybe dipping her fingers in scalding water would keep Jo's mind from woolgathering about Sullivan.

"Toss up some nails, Mooreland," Kavenagh bellowed from his perch atop the rafter.

Sullivan flung the paper sack of hardware into the air. After Jo had informed him of the barn raising this morning, he'd arrived at the blacksmith's property anticipating chaos—kids running underfoot, men arguing and tumbling to their deaths from the top of rafters. So far he'd been the only one to fall off a ladder. In truth, he'd been pleasantly surprised by the well-organized event. The men understood their responsibilities and worked as a team, with Kavenagh the leader.

Another thing that impressed Sullivan was that a framer hadn't been hired. Two clansmen were considered experienced framers and the group relied heavily on their direction. The other men were skilled enough in construction that they were efficient at sawing and pounding boards. Sullivan envied the effortlessness with which they applied their carpenter skills to the project and speculated that their talent derived from their

Scotch-Irish gene pool. Half the men were older than Sullivan, yet possessed the stamina and strength of a man in his twenties. He contemplated the work put into a barn raising two hundred years ago. The preparation must have been extensive—felling trees and fashioning beams, logs and two-by-fours by hand. Fortunately for the clan, the sawmill had donated the wood.

The sun slipped lower in the sky and Sullivan's stomach rumbled.

If he hadn't fed half his lunch to Jeb's hounds, he wouldn't be hungry. *Pesky mutts.* He searched for a glimpse of Jo. They hadn't said more than twenty words to each other since they'd arrived earlier in the morning. As much as he enjoyed helping today, he couldn't wait to spend time alone with her.

This past week, they'd blocked out the world. The clan had ceased to exist. Lightning Jack was a fading memory. Seattle lay a continent away. They'd lived in a make-believe world where nothing mattered but the two of them and their insatiable passion. The first few days Sullivan convinced himself that great sex was the reason for the feelings building inside him. Over a year and half had gone by since his last relationship—if you could call a few dates and a couple of sleepovers a relationship.

Jo was perfect for him. When he was with her, the urge to prove himself disappeared. In her arms he felt worthy. Needed. And even though she never said the words, he felt loved each time she kissed and stroked him. Tonight, he was determined to talk about their relationship.

"Get up here, Mooreland, and give me a hand," Kavenagh shouted, ending Sullivan's musings.

After shifting the ladder several feet sideways, he scaled the rungs, then carefully stepped onto the beam and inched across the joist.

"Can't hold the board. My hands are crampin'." Kavenagh's knuckles were torn and bloodied.

Gripping the wood, Sullivan warned, "You should clean those cuts before they become infected."

"Soon as I finish nailin' this in place." They worked on the support beam for a half hour before Kavenagh announced, "That'll do."

Eyeing the finished roof, Sullivan admitted, "I'm impressed."

"Thanks for helpin' today."

Despite a few aches, pains and blisters Sullivan felt good. Today he'd helped build Kavenagh a barn. Who did his newspaper articles help? His words entertained, even enlightened, but they didn't make a difference in people's lives. He loved the written word. Loved researching facts. Loved uncovering a story angle no one had discovered. He shook off his discontent. He'd worked too damn hard to second-guess his future. He had to remain focused on the editor position, but without Jo and Katie by his side the possible promotion failed to excite him.

"Ms. Macpherson, come quick! Ms. Macpherson!" One of the McKee boys waved his arms at the edge of the woods behind the Kavenagh cabin. "Ms. Macpherson, it's Katie!"

The mention of the little girl's name thrust Sullivan's heart into overdrive. In no time flat, he'd shimmied down the ladder and hit the ground, running for the woods. He'd just passed the cabin when the back door opened and Jo sprinted after him.

"What happened?" he shouted, skidding to a halt in front of the boy.

"Katie fell out of the tree and she can't breathe."

Sullivan didn't wait for Jo to catch up. He grabbed the boy's arm and tugged him into the woods. "Where is she?" He followed the youngster, uncaring that branches swatted his face and vines threatened to trip him. His only concern was reaching Jo's daughter.

They'd sprinted for less than a minute before they broke into a clearing. Several children huddled in a group and Sullivan caught a glimpse of pink—Katie's shoes. He broke through the circle and dropped to his knees.

The child gasped for breath, her eyes wide with fright. Sullivan suspected the fall had scared her silly. In a calming voice, he said, "Tiny breaths. Breathe through your nose. Good girl," he encouraged her when she clamped her lips closed. Sullivan's own heart pumped furiously.

After a few seconds, Katie showed little improvement and Sullivan worried that she might have suffered an internal injury. Before he had the opportunity to examine her, Jo stumbled to their side. "Sweetie, what's wrong?" When Katie didn't respond, Jo's gaze cut to Sullivan.

"She's hyperventilating," he explained, then blocked her arm. "Don't move her. We don't know if she's hurt."

"Let me through. Git now," Granny scolded as she pushed into the growing circle of adults and kids. The old woman crouched near Katie's head. Her gnarled fingers grasped the child's hands and put them against her mouth. "Breathe in…breathe out. Breathe in…breathe out." Slowly Katie's breathing gentled and Granny checked the little girl's head, neck and limbs.

"Is she all right?" Jo's voice trembled.

"Nothin's broke so far as I can tell. She got a bump on her noggin'." Granny brought Jo's hand to the back of Katie's head.

After Jo examined the wound, Sullivan did likewise. "She might have a concussion."

The old woman scowled. "The child's fine. Needs a bit of rest and watchin' is all."

"Would you carry her to the truck?" Jo asked Sullivan.

"Are you crazy? Katie didn't fall and skin her knee. She landed on her head. We've got to call 9-1-1. She might have a hemorrhage, a brain bleed or a fractured skull. Where's the nearest hospital?" He glanced around the group. No one answered.

Fingernails bit into Sullivan's forearm and he frowned at Jo's grasp on his arm. "Granny checked Katie over. We'll keep a close eye on her, and if she doesn't improve in a day or two, I'll take her to a doctor," Jo promised.

"You're going to accept an old woman's word over a medical doctor's? Are you nuts, Jo?" An eerie silence descended upon the woods, but Sullivan pushed his point. "Granny can't see through a skull the way an X-ray or an MRI can. Katie's your daughter. You can't entrust her well-being to some… some…hocus-pocus healer."

Gasps echoed through the group. Not acknowledging the crowd was easier than ignoring the fire spitting from Jo's eyes. After a lengthy silence, Granny crawled to her feet and walked off, her black skirt swishing against her legs. So what if he'd offended her? Katie's life was more important than the old woman's feelings.

"Leave us, Sullivan. I'll carry Katie myself."

Ignoring the steely tone in Jo's voice, he assured her, "If this is about money or not having health insurance, I'll pay her medical bills."

Jo reached for her daughter.

"No." He gently scooped Katie into his arms and cradled her against his chest. "I've got her."

Careful not to stumble, he marched through the woods. Sullivan decided he'd never felt as helpless and frustrated as he did at this moment. Where did a person draw the line between preserving tradition and a person's well-being?

JO CLOSED the door behind her when she stepped out of the house. At the far end of the porch, Sullivan reclined in a rocking chair and stared into the dark. He hadn't moved from the seat since they'd arrived home and he'd taken Katie up to her bed. He'd declined supper, so Jo had left a plate of leftover fried chicken on the table by the chair. He hadn't touched the food.

Swallowing a sigh, she joined him on the porch. Rocking soothed the soul, her mother had claimed. Jo hated that her and Sullivan's idyllic week had arrived at such an abrupt end. Not that she was surprised. She'd learned the hard way that nothing good lasted forever.

"I owe you an apology," he mumbled.

"Not me. Granny. You hurt her feelings by disrespecting her in front of the clan."

Agitated, he vaulted from the chair and shoved a hand through his hair. "When I saw Katie lying on the ground, gasping…"

"I was scared, too, Sullivan," she whispered. Jo doubted she'd be able to close her eyes at night for the next ten years without imagining her daughter struggle for air on the forest floor. And she'd never forget the panic on Sullivan's face as he sprinted into the woods after Katie.

His reaction to the incident confirmed what Jo had refused to acknowledge the past few weeks: Sullivan loved her daughter as if she were his own. But he wasn't a member of the clan, and today proved that some differences were too large to overcome. Sullivan would never place his faith in the clan healer.

He'd journeyed across the States, intending to capture the next big story, but instead had captured her and Katie's hearts. Jo had entertained the idea of a permanent relationship with Sullivan—though her daydreams had never ended like this.

"It's time for you to go, Sullivan."

He faced her, hands clenched at his sides. "What about us?"

Lord, she hadn't expected the end to hurt so much. "There is no us." Their worlds were too diverse for either of them to be happy living in the other's. He'd begged her to trust him and had encouraged her to tell the clan's story to the world. He'd alleged that once people understood the culture they'd insist on helping to preserve the customs and traditions of the clan. Impossible. If the world was full of people like Sullivan, who only wanted to support some of what the clan believed in but not everything, what good would her speeches do?

With all her heart she wished Sullivan wasn't a reporter with his own agenda. He'd been the first man who teased, flattered and loved her the way she dreamed of. She didn't doubt he'd be a terrific father to Katie and she physically ached that she couldn't give her daughter that gift. If only he'd been raised in the Appalachian Mountains, then he'd understand what was at stake for future generations.

"My behavior today may have been out of line, but you shouldn't have taken chances with Katie. For Christ's sake, Jo, she's your flesh and blood."

"My faith in Granny is strong, Sullivan. I trust her with my life and my daughter's."

"You'd place your child in harm's way simply because you feel an allegiance to the old woman?"

Frustration rolled off Sullivan in waves and Jo's throat tightened as she witnessed his struggle to understand. "Our beliefs have been ingrained in us for generations, dating back centuries to when the clan lived along the shores of Scotland. We've always claimed responsibility of our own. Right or wrong, it's our way."

"There was a moment in the woods, Jo, that you hesitated. You almost gave in to taking Katie to a real doctor."

Lest he read the truth in her eyes, Jo glanced away from his probing stare. She confessed that for a fraction of a second her faith in Granny had faltered. She blamed Sullivan. Had he not been present, she wouldn't have doubted Granny's diagnosis.

"In the morning, I'll drive you to the gristmill to retrieve your car."

Silence followed her announcement. When she gathered the courage to look his way, she winced at the tight lines bracketing his mouth.

"What about my story? I'm not leaving for Seattle until I've found Lightning Jack and interviewed him."

"Didn't you propose to focus your article on the clan and—"

"Yes. But in order to be considered for that promotion, I have to bring in an interview with the bootlegger."

The only way to make Sullivan return to Seattle was to give him what he wanted—Lighting Jack. Swallowing the lump lodged in her throat, she instructed, "Meet me at the still at midnight." The knowledge of what she was about to do pained Jo more than she'd anticipated. But she'd do this—for the children. For the next generation of Heather's Hollow.

"We can't leave Katie alone," he argued.

"Granny won't budge from her side. She plans to stay until morning."

"Why the still?" he queried.

"Because that's where Lightning Jack will be."

Chapter Thirteen

Sullivan stood in Jo's yard, facing the cabin, debating whether to meet her at the still. She'd left in the truck an hour earlier—no explanation of where she was headed. After their falling-out, he didn't ask.

The past week an unspoken truce had developed between them. For five days they'd dropped their individual agendas and put their efforts into living for the moment, for each other. Playing and loving like a young couple crazy in lust.

Lust? Or love?

Love. He'd grown up believing the four-letter word *L O V E* was as unspeakable as the F-word. He couldn't recall ever loving anyone, not even his mother. His two longest relationships had lasted about a month. Now he could barely recall the names and personalities of the women. Oh, hell. He'd fallen in love with Johanna Macpherson.

And the idea of walking away from Jo and her daughter created a empty hole in the middle of his chest.

He made his living by the written word, but he struggled to describe his emotions when he made love with Jo. Her gaze softened. Her eyes glowed. Her limbs curled around him as if she'd intended to fuse their bodies. His feelings for Jo, however, went beyond the physical. She embodied traits he admired in a person—strength, determination and courage.

They'd never voiced their feelings—not even during the height of their lovemaking. Their eyes had spoken for them.

This evening he'd replayed the events of the day in his mind, but his reaction to them hadn't changed—if Katie had been his daughter, he'd have rushed her to the nearest hospital or medical clinic. The admission had confirmed what he'd believed but had denied these past weeks: his and Jo's lives were worlds apart, and he wasn't referring to distance. With centuries of customs and beliefs standing between them, there was little chance of meeting in the middle.

The way Jo and Granny had handled Katie's accident had acknowledged what he'd suspected all along—that these people weren't *playing* at being descendants of the Scotch-Irish who'd settled Heather's Hollow. They didn't follow customs when they alleged them convenient or to their benefit. They followed tradition because that was the world they lived in.

The clan was for real.

Jo had tossed down the gauntlet when she'd agreed to introduce him to Lightning Jack—afterward he would no longer have a reason to remain in the hollow. He considered his story—if he included information on the famous bootlegger, he'd lose Jo. If he didn't mention the man, he'd still lose her.

Hell of a choice.

Lightning Jack was the key to the Monterey Award, the key to a promotion to editor. The key to validating what he'd struggled to achieve the past twenty years. Which was to matter. To be respected. To be wanted. To be *somebody*. Yet without Jo by his side, that dream had lost its allure.

Before he'd insulted Granny in the woods, neither Jo nor the other clan members had cared if he was famous or wealthy. As long as he was a decent human being with basic values and morals, he was good enough for the people of Heather's Hollow.

Why wasn't being himself enough? Did he have to devote his whole life to proving he was good, better and best? A part of him wished to remain with the woman he loved and the little girl who'd wiggled her way into his heart. If he hadn't panicked today and spouted off... *Ask for Jo's forgiveness. Make her believe she needs you.*

Yeah, right. Johanna Macpherson didn't need Sullivan the way he needed her. She was the most self-sufficient person he'd ever met.

Katie needs you.

Ah, Katie. His little leprechaun. He couldn't imagine never seeing her again. There was a real yearning in Sullivan to be a part of the child's life. Every boy and girl deserved the love of a mother *and* a father.

Even if he were able to convince Jo to give him a second chance, how would he make a living in the hollow? He had no college degree. No skill or trade that would earn enough money to support a family. The sawmill might be an option, but he'd die of boredom if he couldn't challenge his mind— investigate, research, write stories.

For too many years he'd covered a beat, walked the streets, witnessed change and thrived on the fast-paced action of the city. How would he handle living day in and day out in a place where nothing varied? Where the outside world ceased to exist save for the evening news on television?

He sympathized with Jo's belief that educating the younger generation was vital to preserving the clan's traditions and heritage. What troubled Sullivan was her insistence that the answer to safeguarding their history had to come solely from within the clan. Jo's suspicion of the outside world prevented the clan from receiving potential support. She believed non-

Appalachian people were ignorant of the clan's way. Maybe so. But if Jo educated them and opened the world's eyes, she might be surprised by their reaction.

If he ever met up with that stupid ass, Brian, he'd deck the guy for hurting Jo in college. Her experience with the jerk had made her determined to hide from the world, rather than risk censure or criticism.

Once during the past week, he'd almost asked her and Katie to return to Seattle with him. But he'd chickened out. Jo would never leave her home, her roots. All his life Sullivan had wished for a home. Not an apartment, a room above a liquor store, the back seat of a car or a homeless shelter. If he had a real home, he wouldn't walk away from it, either.

Leaving Jo and Katie would be difficult, but he was grateful they had people who loved them. People who would watch over them.

With a deep breath, he forced his gaze from the house and marched to the trailhead, dread weighing heavy on his shoulders. He was awed that Jo had persuaded Lightning Jack to agree to a meeting but doubted the bootlegger would reveal the whereabouts of his private still. Maybe the old man would agree to a photo. Regardless of the amount of information he'd be able to drag out of the coot, Sullivan was eager to meet the legend Jo would protect with her life.

Tonight, the winds swept down the mountainside and howled through the branches of the maple and oak trees. An omen, perhaps? Sullivan recalled the first day he'd driven the corkscrew road leading into the hollow. He hadn't paid attention to the beauty of the area because he'd been too intent on preventing the Corvette from sliding off the side of the mountain. He'd miss the unique landscape—the high razor-back ridges that plunged into small, remote utopias such as Heather's Hollow.

He comforted himself with the thought that when he completed his story, he'd return to the heart of Appalachia one last time. He was determined to keep his promise that Jo be allowed to read the article before it went to press.

The orange glow of lantern light peeked through the shrubs and underbrush. Keeping to the shadows, he scanned the area. Nothing but darkness danced at the edge of the clearing. The still sat silent, the ashes having been cleared from the stone furnace.

Anticipation pumped through his blood as he stepped beyond the brush and out into the open. He moved a lantern from one of the old tree stumps, figuring Lightning Jack would be more comfortable sitting while he answered questions and reminisced about the old days. Sullivan recalled stories about the famous Hatfields and McCoys. He intended to ask the bootlegger if he'd ever experienced a feud with another family. His clan must have made a few enemies during Prohibition, when moonshiners competed for territory and buyers.

Rustling sounds and footsteps alerted Sullivan that he was no longer alone. An arm poked through the brush, then a body appeared. *What the heck?*

Jo stood in the circle of light. Alone.

"Where's Lightning Jack?" he asked.

Silence.

Disappointment filled Sullivan. "Did he change his mind?"

"A dead man can't change his mind."

Dead? "What do you mean, dead?"

She looked him straight in the eye. "Lightning Jack died two years ago. I've been impersonating him ever since."

She's joking. "You don't have to make up excuses for him. If he refused to meet me, fine."

"I'm telling the truth, Sullivan. Lightning Jack, otherwise known as Robert McCulley, was my late grandfather."

McCulley... Where had he heard that name before? *The church cemetery.*

"Now you have your story, Sullivan. There's no reason to stay."

A pang shot through him, threatening to double him over. She wanted him off the mountain so badly that she'd revealed her grandfather's secret and put herself in great jeopardy in order to get Sullivan to move on.

"The recipe for heather whiskey had been safeguarded by generations of male McCulleys. Grandpa was the last male in the McCulley line. The recipe had never been passed down to a female until me," she explained. "I'm the only female in the clan who's ever brewed the whiskey. I gave Grandpa my promise to carry on the tradition."

"How did your grandfather keep his identity a secret from the clan all those years?"

"He used runners to deliver his whiskey and never dealt with customers face-to-face. There might have been a few clan members over the years who'd suspected my grandfather might be the infamous Lightning Jack, but they wouldn't dare risk bringing bad luck to the hollow by uttering their suspicions."

"You lied to me." The realization shouldn't hurt, but his chest tightened painfully. "You don't brew whiskey for the clan, do you?"

Her gaze slid to the ground. "No. I sell moonshine illegally."

"You'd knowingly break the law just to keep your grandfather's legend alive?"

"I need the money to support the school. The clan doesn't pay me a salary and all the supplies, computers and costs associated with the school are paid by me."

"Damn." He should have suspected as much after Jo had mentioned that the clan didn't pay their church pastor, but he'd had other things on his mind that afternoon. Refusing to become distracted by the memories of their lovemaking, he spat,

"Don't people question where you're getting the money to run the school?"

"The clan elders know I'm selling moonshine under the guise of Lightning Jack, but they won't divulge my secret. Nor will they ever bring the subject up in conversation. The rest of the clan might wonder, but people won't ask."

Appalachian attitude—keep to yourself and don't poke your nose into your neighbor's business. "So the clan members never figured out your grandfather and Lightning Jack were one and the same?"

"Right."

"And everyone believes Lightning Jack is still alive?"

"Like I said, only the elders know the truth."

"What happens if you get caught, Jo?"

"I won't." She raised a hand when he began to object. "But if I do, then it will be Johanna Macpherson caught moonshining, not Lightning Jack."

"Eventually people are going to wonder how it's possible for Lightning Jack to still be alive and able to make whiskey. Why not tell people that your grandfather was the infamous bootlegger? Explain that he left you the recipe and you're carrying on the tradition."

She shook her head. "The older generation is suspicious of women making moonshine. As long as my customers believe Lightning Jack is the brewer, they'll continue to buy from me."

"Aren't they surprised when a woman delivers the stuff?"

"Not really. I've made deliveries for my grandpa— Lightning Jack, that is—for years. Before I'd gone away to college and then again when I'd returned."

"I can't believe your grandfather's runners didn't figure out that he was the famous moonshine maker."

"My father or one of the elders would take the whiskey to a drop-off location where the runners waited."

"Sounds stupidly simple."

"Appalachian folk aren't complicated the way city dwellers are."

Sullivan sat on a tree stump and studied the dirt under his shoes. "I must have been a constant source of amusement for you and the elders when I insisted on interviewing Lighting Jack."

"Amusement, no. Frustration, yes." The corner of Jo's mouth tilted in a semblance of a smile.

As an only child who'd lost her parents and grandmother, Jo must have been close to the old man, especially after working with him for years. Forcing aside his anger, he asked, "How did your grandfather die?"

"In his sleep. I found him in the fishing cabin."

What a fool he'd been, chasing a man who no longer existed. What the hell was he going to tell his editor in chief? "I guess there's no reason to stay." *Say something, Jo. Tell me you don't want me to go.*

A tear leaked from Jo's eye, the drop glistening in the lantern light. "There's nothing left here for you," she whispered, her voice cracking.

That one tear crushed him. He'd never witnessed Jo cry, not even when Katie had been injured. That she'd shed a tear for him... "Soon, Johanna Macpherson, you're going to have to face your greatest fear."

Chin high, she snapped, "What might that be?"

"Leaving your mountain." He had to get out of there before he unloaded his hurt and frustration and said things he'd regret. Heart pounding irregularly—as if the organ were broken or injured—he muttered, "I'll be ready to go at daylight." He paused, his back to her. "And don't worry. Your precious secret is safe with me."

BROKENHEARTED.

There was no other word to describe Jo's pain. The end of June was right around the corner. Four weeks had passed since Sullivan had left the hollow and not one word from him. He hadn't even had the decency to inform her that he'd safely arrived in Seattle. After all they'd been through together…after making love…she deserved at least a phone call.

"The squirrel babies playing, Mama?" Katie asked from her seat at the table, where she worked on a bowl of ice cream.

Several times her daughter had caught Jo daydreaming out the kitchen window and Jo had come up with the excuse that she was watching the squirrels play. She didn't want Katie to know that she checked the tree house, hoping she'd catch Sullivan standing under the big maple. "Not anymore, honey." Disgusted with herself for allowing Sullivan to steal her every other passing thought, she tossed aside the dish towel and joined her daughter at the table. "Granny's going to stay the next couple of nights with us."

"How come she's sleeping at our cabin so much?"

"Granny's lonely," Jo fibbed. She'd been brewing overtime the past couple of weeks in order to prepare a double order of moonshine for the Roswell clan's July Fourth reunion. In truth, she looked forward to working the still. She hadn't been able to sleep since Sullivan had left—too many dreams. Each morning she'd wake tired, lonely and frustratingly aroused. Dark circles smudged the skin beneath her eyes and she'd become addicted to pop, thanks to the Dr Pepper that Sullivan hadn't drunk before he'd left.

"When's Mr. Sully coming back?" Katie's question ended another episode of daydreaming.

"Honey, I told you Sullivan went home to Seattle."

Katie rolled her eyes. "But he told me he has to come back

so you can read the—" her brow scrunched, then she flashed a chocolate smile "—the story he's gonna write."

If Sullivan hadn't called after all this time, then Jo doubted he'd fulfill his promise and bring her the article to read. She may have injured his pride and hurt his feelings by insisting he leave the hollow, but he'd never betray her and reveal the truth about Lightning Jack. She believed Sullivan cared enough about her and Katie not to use them for personal gain. Sadly, comfort made for a cold bedfellow.

"Mr. Sully may not have time to visit again."

Call it a gut feeling, but Jo suspected she'd seen the last of Sullivan when she'd dropped him off at the gristmill to retrieve the Corvette. Amos, bless his heart, had washed and waxed the vehicle and cleaned the white walls. Sullivan had praised Amos and thanked him, but there'd been no excitement in his voice. No sparkle in his eye. *Because of you.*

"Mama?"

"What, baby?"

"Do you miss, Mr. Sully?"

More than you know, sweetie. "Yes." Sullivan was naive in Appalachian ways, but eager and thirsty for knowledge about the hollow. Determined, even stubborn. Tender and patient with Katie. Kind to Jeb's hounds. Willing to pitch in and help at the barn raising. And loving—sweet kisses, heated touches. But the one trait missing from her list—one Sullivan didn't stand a chance of acquiring—was unconditional acceptance of the clan's ways.

Yet, she felt Sullivan truly wanted to understand her Appalachian life. *Maybe that's enough, Jo. Maybe that's all you should ask of him. He doesn't have to agree with everything as long as he respects your choices.*

A truck engine sputtered up the drive. "Granny's here," Katie squealed, and made a dash for the door.

Thank goodness for Granny. After Jo's parents and grandmother had passed away, she'd sought out the clan healer for support and guidance. Was it her imagination, or was Granny walking slower, her shoulders hunched, feet dragging. Jo ushered the older woman inside and seated her at the kitchen table. While she fetched her guest a glass of lemonade, she reminded Katie, "Time to feed Jelly."

As soon as her daughter filled the dog bowl with food and went out to the porch, Jo grasped Granny's hand and scooted her chair closer. "Something's wrong. What is it?"

Green eyes, faded with time, stared unseeingly across the kitchen.

"You're scaring me, Granny. Are you feeling poorly?"

"It's Catherine."

Catherine? For a moment Jo didn't recognize the name, then she remembered—Granny's teenage daughter who'd gotten pregnant and run off with the baby's father. "What about her?"

Gnarled fingers squeezed Jo's hand. "Catherine's dead."

Jo gasped. "How? When?"

"Got a letter from Catherine's daughter, Maggie."

"Maggie? Your granddaughter is named after you?" Jo hoped Granny would find comfort in that knowledge. Jo's mother had told her years ago that Granny and Catherine, both headstrong females, had had a tumultuous relationship. No one had been surprised when the teen had run away. Jo suspected Granny had assumed one day her daughter would show up in the hollow, but the young girl hadn't—and now, she never would.

Tears pooled in Granny's eyes. "Catherine died of cancer."

"Oh, Granny, I'm sorry." Jo wrapped her arms around bony shoulders. "Is your granddaughter planning to visit you?"

"Didn't say."

"Maybe you should invite her. She'll need family and—"

"Catherine died six months ago and my granddaughter didn't care to write me then." The old woman's lip quivered.

"I won't go to the still tonight," Jo stated.

"Go on. Watchin' Katie will keep me from thinkin' 'bout Catherine."

Jo hated leaving the old woman to grieve alone. "You're sure?"

"Sure as I'm sure yer wastin' time." She clutched Jo's arm. "Be careful. Bad news comes in threes."

Granny was suspicious, more so than the younger generation. But Jo acknowledged that Kavenagh's barn fire was the first bad event; now the news of Granny's daughter having died was the second. Hopefully the third event was a long time off. "I'll be careful."

JO TREKKED along the path leading to the still, unable to shake off the premonition that a monumental event was about to occur. No one ignored Granny's warnings, so this evening Jo toted a shotgun.

Her body shivered at the memory of the night she'd transported the moonshine to Earl Payton and encountered the strange man on the road. In a few days, Jo would make another delivery to the Payton farm…

Maybe the thief was the least of her worries. What if this time she lost control of the truck and it plunged off the mountainside? In all the years she'd driven the trail, only once had she had a close call. Snow had covered the road and she'd misjudged the curve. The spirits of the clan had been guarding her that night, because she'd spun the wheel in the nick of time, saving herself—along with a couple thousand dollars of whiskey—from an early grave at the bottom of the Black River.

The news of Catherine's death confirmed how precious life was, which made her question why she put herself in danger each month driving the treacherous route. Her daughter deserved better from Jo. She should expect better from herself, too. She thought of her grandfather and how proud he would be that she'd safeguarded the family recipe, but she suspected he'd be deeply distressed if he knew she was putting herself at risk.

All this time she'd convinced herself that she needed the money for the school and to support herself and Katie. But that was only part of the truth. Tears burning her eyes, she admitted that she kept making moonshine because she wanted to keep her grandfather's spirit alive. He'd been the one steadying force in her life.

After his death, Jo had felt abandoned and scared. Robert McCulley's passing had left a terrible void in her life. Instead of moving on, she'd felt it easier to assume his role as a moonshiner and pretend he'd never died. She'd convinced herself that her grandfather would have wished her to continue selling whiskey to his customers, when in truth Lightning Jack would never have wanted Jo to do such a thing.

Tonight would be the beginning of the end of her commercial bootlegging. She'd inform Earl when she visited him in a few days that there would be no more heather whiskey. Jo was certain speculation of Lightning Jack's death would follow. So be it. The time had come to move on. To accept her grandfather's death. To be the mother Katie deserved. And she had Sullivan to thank for making her face the truth.

When she arrived at the still, she focused on the business of brewing. After lighting the lanterns, she studied the area. Nothing appeared disturbed. Satisfied the equipment remained as she'd left it the previous night, she began a fire in the stone furnace. While she stirred the boiling mash, she mulled over the idea of seeking Sullivan's forgiveness. And if she could find the courage, she'd ask for his help in obtaining legitimate funding for the school.

A branch snapping caught Jo's attention and her heart climbed into her throat. Eyes narrowed, she searched the blackness beyond the firelight. Her shoulders itched—a sign eyes were observing. *Knock it off. Don't allow Granny's words to unnerve you.*

Taking a deep breath, she gathered bunches of heather she'd picked days ago and placed the flower heads in water to simmer, then checked on the mash. In less than a half hour the barrels began collecting steam and condensing the alcohol.

Satisfied all was progressing well, Jo rested on the old tree stump, the rifle lying across her thighs. She resisted the temptation to snooze. Time slowed to a crawl. Minutes passed. Her breathing relaxed and some of the tension eased from her body.

Click.

The quiet noise sounded like an explosion in the clearing. Jo inched her thumb over the trigger.

"Wouldn't do that if I were you, lady," a husky voice warned from the shadows.

Lady? A Yorkie had wandered into her camp. Only a northerner would say *lady.* Jo shifted her gaze in the direction of the warning. Nothing but darkness beyond the lantern light. *Shit fire and thunderation!* as her grandfather would say. "Who are you and what do you want?"

"Put the gun down, miss." A second voice, this time from behind her, ordered.

She didn't dare toss aside her weapon. Whoever the trespassers were, they might want more than her whiskey. Sweat beaded across her upper lip as she considered her options. Run? Chances were they'd grab her or shoot her before she vacated the circle. Fire a round of buckshot into the woods and attempt to scare them off? They'd shoot her dead before she pulled the trigger. Diplomacy was her best option. "What do you want?" She cursed the tremor in her voice.

"Get rid of the gun and we'll talk."

"No, sirree." She stood and pointed toward the voice in front of her, hoping the intruder behind her wouldn't shoot her in the back.

"Calm down, miss. We don't want to hurt you."

"Step into the light. I'd hate to mistake you for the bear that's been roaming these woods the past few months."

A throat cleared, followed by thirty seconds of whispering. Then the bushes rustled and a man moved into the light. Dressed in a deputy's uniform. Good Lord, the law had found her still. "Are you Johanna Macpherson?"

"I am."

His expression turned apologetic. "I have a warrant for your arrest, miss."

Violent tremors racked her body, but she refused to lower her weapon. "Arrest for what?"

More rustling and another man, then another and finally another moved into view, each aiming a handgun at her. "They're DEA, ma'am. Drug Enforcement Administration—"

"I know what the letters stand for," Jo spat. "What do they want with me?"

"You're being arrested for the illegal manufacture and sale of alcohol."

"My whiskey is used for private consumption. It's not for sale." The sideways glances of the DEA agents suggested they saw through the lie.

"We have proof otherwise, ma'am." The deputy's gaze cut between her and the other agents.

"What proof?" she demanded.

"Put the gun down, lady, and we'll talk." The tallest of the agents stepped forward, then froze when Jo trained her shotgun on him.

"Who ratted me out?" she demanded.

The deputy moved in front of Jo. "Answer her question before something happens here that you boys can't explain to your superiors."

At least the deputy had half a brain. Although Jo didn't recognize him, she suspected he'd been raised in the mountains.

"Information about you and your bootlegging activities was passed on to the authorities by the *Seattle Courier* newspaper in Seattle, Washington."

Sullivan? He wouldn't turn her in. The man who'd built her daughter a tree house couldn't be capable of such a betrayal, could he? Numbness seeped into her bones, and with shaking hands, Jo aimed the shotgun at the ground.

Caught up in memories, she didn't protest when the deputy removed the rifle from her grasp. Images of her and Sullivan making love, of quiet talks and their solemn goodbye floated through her mind in slow motion as the DEA agents surrounded her. Sullivan had played her for a fool. Humiliation threatened to make her vomit but she swallowed hard and faced the deputy. "Where are you taking me?"

"To the Perry County Jail in Hazard."

"My daughter's at home. I have to make sure she's looked after."

"You can call from the jail—"

"We'll stop at your cabin," the deputy promised.

"Cuff her," one of the men demanded.

"My patrol car is parked a quarter mile east of the path." The deputy stared into her eyes. "There's no need for handcuffs, is there?"

"No." Jo wouldn't try to escape and risk getting shot. She was all Katie had left in the world. Shame filled Jo when she imagined telling her daughter that she'd been arrested for breaking the law. That her mama was a criminal.

"Her word isn't worth crap," an agent complained.

The deputy faced the others. "You boys aren't from this neck of the woods, so you wouldn't understand our Appalachian ways. Her word is worth her weight in gold."

The deputy tightened his grip on Jo's arm. "You fellows go on now and take your pictures. Make sure you douse the fire and put out the lanterns. We'll meet up at the sheriff's office."

Deputy at her side, Jo marched off, acknowledging that Granny had been right. Bad things did happen in threes.

Chapter Fourteen

Sullivan Mooreland sat at his desk, shooting rubber bands at the computer monitor in the newsroom of the *Seattle Courier*. Ringing telephones and clicking keyboards didn't distract him from acknowledging how lonely he was—a strange feeling for a man who up until now had never experienced such an emotion.

He missed Katie's sweet smile. Jeb's pesky hounds and Kavenagh's conversation. Even Granny's shotgun.

But mostly he yearned for *Jo*. He'd expected to miss her—just not this much. Their lovemaking had blown him away. And the talking about the clan—their hopes, dreams and desires—had touched him deeply. The little boy who'd experienced a crummy childhood reveled in the stories of Jo's early years in the hollow.

Each night when Sullivan entered his sterile, cold apartment, he imagined Jo's cozy cabin, the smell of rolls baking in the oven and Jelly waiting on the porch for Katie to feed him. Here in Seattle, the honking horns and police sirens had once lulled him to sleep. Now the racket caused Sullivan sleep deprivation. He lay in bed at night straining to identify a cricket chirp, a bird tweet or the roar of the wind whistling down the mountain. Eventually he drifted off, only to be plagued by dreams of Jo.

A glance over his shoulder confirmed that the editor in chief remained occupied on the phone. Sullivan had been waiting all morning for a verdict on the feature article he'd written for the paper. Much to his boss's dismay, Sullivan had taken weeks, not days, to compile a seven-part exposé on Appalachian culture. He'd honored his promise to Jo and not divulged her grandfather's identity or information on Jo's bootlegging activities.

He suspected that without Lightning Jack, the article didn't stand a chance of winning the coveted Monterey Award.

He didn't care.

His battle with insomnia had led to numerous episodes of soul-searching in the darkest hours before dawn. He'd realized that he'd wasted years attempting to prove his worth, striving for awards and recognition, when all along what he really wanted in life was to be loved. To be important not to everyone, but to one special person. Maybe the clan had rubbed off on him, because he no longer gave a crap about what the rest of the world thought of him. Only one person's opinion mattered—Jo's.

When the chief okayed the rough draft, Sullivan intended to return to Kentucky and present Jo the opportunity to read the article before it went to press. Her endorsement was important to Sullivan. He hoped she'd appreciate the thorough research he'd done on the story.

Once he received her consent, he wanted to discuss his idea for a book on the life and history of the Scotch-Irish clan of Heather's Hollow. He'd written an outline and proposal but refused to submit the material to an agent or publisher until he spoke with Jo. He hoped to talk her into coauthoring the project with him.

Collaborating on a book would provide him with an excuse to spend more time in Heather's Hollow with Jo and Katie. If he was fortunate, he'd earn Jo's forgiveness and she'd allow him a chance to prove that the life they could create together would be better than anything they'd ever do alone. He wasn't going to let Jo walk away without a fight. He worried about her safety—toiling at the still and transporting moonshine alone at night.

On the chance they sold their book and it became a huge success and gained the attention of the masses, Jo would have an opportunity as none other to convince people to preserve one of America's last bits of living history. With time, she would discover that not everyone—

"Get in here, Mooreland," the editor in chief bellowed. The boss was miffed—hopefully at the person he'd been conversing with on the phone and not Sullivan.

Despite the chief's irritation, calmness filled Sullivan as he strolled into the office. He understood that his failure to bring in a story about Lightning Jack killed his chances of snagging the promotion to editor. Fine by him. His days at the paper were numbered. If Jo agreed to write the book, he intended to leave Seattle for good. "What's up?"

"Close the door."

The boss's dark scowl terrified interns, but the bulldog expression no longer fazed Sullivan.

"Sit."

After moving a pile of newspapers from the chair to the floor, Sullivan slouched on the seat.

"I mailed your feature story to the Monterey Award committee."

"What?" Sullivan popped off the cushion. Jo would never forgive him if he didn't keep his promise. "That was a rough draft."

"Revisions wouldn't have made the story better. It was the worst piece of crap you've written in years." While Howard droned on about the article having no meat—meaning Lightning Jack—Sullivan made a mental note to contact the Monterey Award committee and withdraw his entry.

"Mooreland, you with me?"

"Not anymore, Howard."

There was a burst of laughter, followed by, "Good one, Mooreland." When Sullivan didn't crack a smile, the chief's expression sobered and his gray eyes turned hard. "You claimed you hadn't obtained an interview with the bootlegger after damn near a month among those hillbillies." He stood, leaned across his desk and stared Sullivan straight in the eye. "Call it a hunch, but I suspect you were lying."

Sweat beaded Sullivan's forehead. That was his story, his investigation, and he could do with it what he wanted.

"Ed mentioned in passing that you'd been burning the midnight oil—"

"Ed should have kept his mouth shut."

"He did you a big favor." Howard grinned. "I took the liberty of doing a bit of investigating myself and uncovered your information on Lightning Jack."

Sullivan clenched his jaw until he feared his teeth would crack.

"I should fire your ass for hiding the real story."

Furious, Sullivan slammed his palm against the desk, startling the other man. "Damn you, Howard. What did you do with that information?"

"You've lost your edge, Mooreland. Did something happen between you and that Macpherson woman?"

"Johanna Macpherson is none of your business."

"You broke the cardinal rule of reporting—got involved with the subject of your story." Howard shook his head, disgust deepening the wrinkles across his forehead. "The real story was that woman impersonating her grandfather, Lightning Jack, and carrying on his bootlegging legacy."

"It's *my* story. *My* decision how I cover it," Sullivan insisted.

"Wrong. You're an employee of the newspaper. That story belongs to me."

Hands fisted at his sides, Sullivan demanded, "Who did you pass the information to?"

"I've got connections with the DEA. They were very interested."

DEA?

Howard tossed Sullivan's project across the desk. "Rewrite it, and this time include the woman's arrest."

Heart slamming against his rib cage, Sullivan demanded, "What do you mean, arrest? What's happened to Jo? Where is she?"

"She's sitting in a cell in the Perry County jail in Hazard, awaiting arraignment."

"How long has she been in custody?"

"Two weeks."

"Shit! And you're telling me this now?" Fearing he'd slug the man, Sullivan backed away from the desk. "I knew you were ruthless, but this time you've crossed the line."

"That's always been your problem, Mooreland—you're afraid to cross the line and nab the real story."

Sick to his gut, he sneered, "I'll give you a *real* story. Wait until America reads how one editor in chief's greed has ruined the lives of innocent people and sent to jail a woman whose only concern has been saving her clan's heritage."

Howard sputtered, "You wouldn't dare—"

"Hell, yes, I'd dare. That's one line I am willing to cross." He smirked. "How many subscribers will the paper lose when readers discover the editor in chief handed over an innocent woman to the law for the sake of journalistic sensationalism?"

"You're fired, Mooreland. Clear your desk and get the hell out."

"You can't fire me. Remember? I already quit!" Positive he'd explode if he didn't leave the building ASAP, he strode from the office, slamming the door behind him. He marched to his desk, ignoring all but one of the stunned stares of his colleagues—Ed. "You betrayed me, damn you," Sullivan accused.

Ed swallowed hard and glanced away.

"What's the matter? Can't look me in the eye?" When the reporter remained mute, Sullivan added, "I trusted you. This is how you repay years of loyalty and friendship?"

"You don't understand," Ed pleaded. "I need that editor position more than you do. I've got four kids to feed and a wife nagging at me because there's never enough money."

"And that gave you the right to turn over information that sent a woman to jail? My God, she's a single mother with a six-year-old daughter depending on her." Fury escalated inside him when he pictured Jo sitting behind bars, wearing an orange jumpsuit. So help him God, he had to make this right.

"I didn't give him the file. Howard searched your desk."

"You're a pathetic excuse for a man." Ed's face reddened and Sullivan hoped to hell the reporter would take a swing at him, because he was itching for a fight. After years of busting his butt, this was his reward? He glanced around the newsroom, viewing the place for the first time through different eyes, the eyes of a man who no longer intended to put himself first in his life. Realizing that the reporters, seemingly working together, were in reality pitted against one another. Competing for the next big story. The next promotion.

He'd been one of them—eager, greedy, manipulative. Whether Jo forgave him or not, Sullivan acknowledged his reporting days were over. He was through using other people's misfortune to his advantage.

"Sullivan, I'm sorry. I didn't think you cared—"

"Well, you're wrong, Ed. I care about that clan in Kentucky. As a matter of fact, I fell in love with Johanna Macpherson."

His friend's face drained of color.

"I'd planned to ask her to marry me. Now I'll be lucky if she doesn't shoot me on sight." Grabbing only his Rolodex, contact file and copies of the stories he'd written for the paper, he added a parting shot, "Hope it was worth our friendship." He stormed out of the newsroom, and rode the elevator to the underground-parking garage. Not until he sat in his car did he allow all his emotions to surface. With shaking hands he gripped the steering wheel.

That Jo was locked in a jail cell threatened to make him physically ill. He'd brought nothing but misery to her life. He'd been careless and had made a rookie mistake by leaving his notes lying around. The only explanation—not excuse— he could come up with was that he hadn't been himself since leaving Kentucky.

Jo hadn't phoned him after she'd been arrested, and it spoke volumes about her opinion of him. In her mind he was positive she believed he'd behaved in typical flatlander fashion—with ignorance. She wouldn't trust him, but she would trust her clan. *Appalachian people take care of their own.*

Jo's words played over and over in his mind as he navigated the streets to his apartment. He pictured Katie's face and worried about who was watching the little girl. Was she frightened without her mother?

When he keyed into his apartment, he called Jo's cell phone. After several rings he got her voice mail. He hung up without leaving a message. Hoping that a neighbor was keeping an eye on Katie, he dialed the cabin.

On the tenth ring, Granny picked up the phone. "If a person

ain't answered in three rings, means they don't want to jabber with ya."

"Granny, don't hang up. This is Sullivan Mooreland."

Silence. "I'm concerned about Jo—"

"Well, ya fer sure should be. Ya done slipped the noose 'round her neck. Ya callin' to find out when the hangin' is?"

He deserved every cruel word the old woman spouted. "Granny…" He swallowed the rest of his protest. It didn't matter who had turned Jo in; he remained at fault. "Tell me where she's being held." He needed confirmation. He didn't trust his boss.

"She's in the Perry County Jail in Hazard."

"Who's looking after Katie?"

"We all are, ya bumpkin."

"Tell Katie that I'm on my way to Kentucky and I'm going to get her mother out of jail." When Granny didn't respond, he added, "I'm hopping a flight this afternoon. I'll be there early tomorrow morning."

Fearing his message wouldn't be passed on, he promised, "I'm going to make this right, Granny." He hung up and made a flight reservation, then fished Dean Saunders's business card from his wallet. Years ago, he'd written a feature story on the activist lawyer in San Francisco. Sullivan was positive the man would help Jo.

Dean had made a name for himself when he'd defended a group of environmentalists who'd protested developers ripping into the redwoods in northern California. These days Saunders flew all over the country representing clients. Sullivan left his contact information with Saunders's assistant, then packed his bags and headed to the airport.

Contrary to what Granny believed, no way was Sullivan leaving Jo to hang out to dry after what his boss had done. After what *he'd* done.

SULLIVAN STOOD outside the Perry County Jail in Hazard, Kentucky, and decided he'd landed in the middle of a scene from a Dr Seuss movie—*Hillbilly Jamboree*. One square city block had been barricaded off out of necessity. Tents had been erected in the middle of the street; lounge chairs and card tables were scattered along the sidewalk. Truck beds containing barbecues, couches and coolers occupied the parking spaces out front. A fiddle band played on the steps of the jail, and a hot-dog vender opened for business on the corner.

Kids skipped rope, played tag and threw Frisbees on the grass adjacent to the jail. Hanging from the lower limbs of the maple trees lining the street were teenage boys firing grapes from homemade slingshots at law officers entering and exiting the building. And amid all this chaos a large group of adults formed a picket line, carrying signs that read: Free the Teacher, Bootleggers Have Rights, Too, and Save Appalachia.

He searched for a familiar face but didn't see Granny, Kavenagh, Amos or Betty Sue—no one from Finnegan's Stand or Heather's Hollow.

"What the hell is going on here?" Dean Saunders spoke. Briefcase in hand, the rotund man mopped his sweaty brow with a white handkerchief and gaped at the rambunctious gathering.

"I believe this is the Appalachian way of coming to the aid of one of their own."

Saunders pulled out his cell phone. "I don't understand why the media aren't all over this." He turned in a slow circle, then spoke into the phone. "Gloria. Orchestrate a media blitz on Johanna Macpherson. Perry County Jail, Hazard, Kentucky. TV, Internet and radio. And make it happen five minutes ago."

Whether Jo wished it or not, she and her neighbors were about to go nationwide. "C'mon. I'll introduce you to Jo." Sullivan maneuvered through the throng, ignoring the distrustful stares of the older people, the curious glances of the younger crowd and the grape that thunked him in the back of the head.

"Help you, gentlemen?" a sheriff's deputy inquired when Sullivan and Saunders entered the jail. The law officer rested his boots atop the desk and fiddled with a Rubik's Cube.

"Dean Saunders. I'm here to represent Johanna Macpherson."

Size-twelve feet smacked against the floor. "About time she got a lawyer." He tossed aside the toy. "How'd you get her to agree to let you take the case?" The deputy shook hands with Saunders. "Butch Baker."

"She's not aware that I'm representing her," Saunders answered. "This is Sullivan Mooreland, a friend of Ms. Macpherson's."

The young deputy's eyes bulged. "I recollect hearin' your name a time or two."

Sullivan didn't doubt a cussword accompanied his name whenever someone spoke it.

The deputy leaned forward and muttered, "Between you and me, them DEA agents is chompin' at the bit 'cause their case stalled out."

"Stalled out how?" Saunders asked.

"Can't charge her with nothin' 'cause no one's talkin'. Can't find a witness to admit they bought her moonshine." He grinned. "She claims she was makin' whiskey for personal consumption."

"Then why is she sitting in jail?" Sullivan asked.

Butch eyed Sullivan. "Claims she's waitin' on a big-city newspaper reporter. She's got a story to tell and she's not leavin' till she tells it."

Sullivan's eyes burned so badly that he had to pretend interest in the Most Wanted poster tacked to the corkboard on the wall. He was beyond grateful for whatever made Jo decide to allow him a chance to explain—but he was under no illusion she'd forgive him.

"'Sides," Butch continued, "the sheriff's daddy and Ms. Macpherson's granddaddy were real good friends when they were alive. Sheriff said she can stay as long as she wants."

"I'll check over the DEA's paperwork and make sure everything's in order, then I'll speak to the media outside." Saunders rested his briefcase on the deputy's desk and grinned. "I'll warm up the crowd for you two."

"I'm sorry you had to travel—"

"Not a problem. This is a great PR opportunity for me, as well."

"Cell's that way." Butch pointed to the far side of the room. "Door's open."

Sullivan entered the hall, expecting to find a woman in an orange jumpsuit, sitting on the end of a cot, face pale, hair limp, shoulders slumped—total dejection.

Instead he found the cell crowded with clan members. Katie was sprawled on the concrete floor, drawing chalk pictures with Tommy and Bobby. Jo, Annie, Kavenagh and Jeb were seated at a card table, playing a hand of poker. Knitting needles clicking away, Granny rocked in a chair that reminded him of the one on Jo's front porch.

He wasn't sure how long he'd stood staring before Katie spotted him and squealed, "Mama, Mr. Sully's here!" She vaulted off the floor and raced out of the cell, almost knocking Sullivan to his feet when she threw herself at his knees. He reacted out of instinct—lifting her high in the air. "There's my Katie bug." Skinny arms squeezed his neck and he wrapped the child in a fierce bear hug. Lord, he'd missed the little imp. She smelled of sunshine and sweetness. He closed his eyes and absorbed her warmth, grateful beyond measure that Jo hadn't badmouthed him to her daughter.

"'Bout time you got yer sorry ass back here," Kavenagh grumped, scooting his chair away from the table.

Sullivan attempted to release Katie, but she played monkey and clung to his neck, so he propped her on his hip and shook Kavenagh's hand. He'd yet to make eye contact with Jo, afraid once he did he'd embarrass himself by dropping to his knees and begging forgiveness in front of everyone. Annie, flashing a sour expression, pried Katie from his hold by promising, "Time for ice cream." She waved to her sons. "Come on, boys."

One by one they shuffled out of the cell. Granny paused in the hallway, her gaze cutting between him and the shotgun propped against the wall behind the rocker. Sullivan nodded at the old woman's warning—*treat Jo right or get a gut full of buckshot.* Finally alone with Jo, Sullivan pulled in a deep breath and looked at her.

His throat tightened. Her eyes were bluer, more brilliant than he'd remembered. She wore her long red hair in a ponytail, the strands hanging over one shoulder. Dressed in overalls and a red T-shirt, she'd never looked more beautiful. "Jo…" He swallowed hard. Apologizing wasn't the problem, but asking for a second chance terrified him.

"Sullivan." She motioned to the chair across from her.

Nerves taut, he entered the cell and sat. He tapped his fingers against the table, searching for the right words.

"Stop." She stayed his hand.

Automatically he threaded his fingers through hers and squeezed. She didn't pull away and he accepted that as a sign of her willingness to hear his side of the story—more than he deserved.

"I didn't betray you, Jo. Please believe me." He maintained eye contact, praying she'd read the truth in his gaze.

After a long moment, she sighed. "Then tell me how I ended up in here."

Grateful for the opportunity to explain, Sullivan shared the details of his return to the newspaper—writing the article, his intention to allow Jo to read the story before going to press, his boss's unethical actions in confiscating Sullivan's notes and submitting the information to the DEA. "I'm sorry, Jo. I should have safeguarded that information better."

"I believe you, Sullivan." Jo slipped her hand from his.

That was it? No cursing, no shouting, no yelling—just a steady stare confirming the truth in her words—*I believe you*. Encouraged, he confessed, "I learned a lot about myself during my stay with you and Katie—both good and bad." This was more difficult than he'd expected.

"I'm prejudiced. Or I was. I had preconceived ideas about Appalachian people when I arrived in the hollow. You opened my eyes, Jo. You and the others forced me to admit how unfair my thoughts and opinions were." He abandoned his seat and paced the tiny cell. "I came to the conclusion that my criticism of the clan and their way of life was a direct result of jealousy."

Eyes wide, she murmured, "I don't understand."

"Your way of life represents all I've ever wanted. Security. Peace. Love. A real home." Leaning against the far wall, he crossed his arms over his chest. "I criticized you and the clan because I was envious. I've spent my whole adult life trying to be a person others envy."

When Jo didn't comment, he continued, "You showed me that the clan folk are secure in who they are. They don't need to prove themselves to anyone. They take one day at a time, cherish their family and don't compete with their neighbors." He studied the tips of his shoes. "Yes, I'm envious. I've wasted years searching for everything you already have."

Jo left the table and stood before Sullivan. She ached to throw herself into his arms the way her daughter had, but first she had a few things to get off her chest. "Part of me wants to remain angry with you. But I can't."

Permitting her to witness the misery in his brown eyes and the dark circles beneath, he held her gaze. She suspected she'd slept better in the cell than Sullivan had in his Seattle apartment.

"I refused to believe you when you insisted that I had to teach others about our way of life and not just the clan's children. I suspect I knew you were right, but I was terrified of being ridiculed." Sullivan smoothed a hand over her hair, the gentle gesture tweaking her heart.

"When word spread of my arrest and people I'd never met arrived to support me, I was forced to acknowledge that my goal to save the clan was selfish. The folks out there—" she pointed to the barred window in the cell "—are the heart of Appalachia. I have to tell their story in order to tell our clan's." She took a deep breath. "I've remained in jail because I'm terrified of going out there alone." Clasping his face between her hands, she declared, "I can't do this by myself. I need you, Sullivan."

He tucked her against him. "I'll do anything for you, Jo. I was damn scared you wouldn't forgive me."

Reveling in the strength of his hold, she admitted, "At first, I did presume you'd betrayed me. But Granny suggested that a man who would build a tree house for a little girl wouldn't turn against the girl's mother."

Sullivan chuckled. "I never thought Granny would be on my side."

"Was there another reason you returned besides to apologize?" she hinted.

"Yeah. I love you, Johanna Macpherson, warrior queen of Heather's Hollow. I want to be a part of yours and Katie's life if you'll let me."

Heart racing, she whispered, "How much a part?"

Sullivan dropped to one knee and clasped her hand in his. "Johanna Macpherson, will you marry me and let me love you the rest of my life?"

Tears flooded her eyes. "What about Katie?"

"I'd be honored to adopt her and be her father."

Jo's heart swelled. "I love you, too, Sullivan." She wasn't naive enough to think love alone would solve the world's or the clan's troubles, but Sullivan's love would make life sweeter, dearer and more fulfilling.

"Good Lord, girl, will ya answer the man?" Granny grumbled, standing outside the cell with the rest of the gang, gawking and grinning.

"Yes, Sullivan. I will marry you and—" She glanced at her daughter. "Katie, would you like Sullivan to be your daddy?"

Her daughter's eyes rounded. "You wanna be my daddy, Mr. Sully?"

"Yes, Katie. I'd be proud to be your father."

Katie dashed into the cell, and Sullivan lifted her into his arms for a group hug.

"That's a definite yes." Jo laughed at her daughter's enthusiasm.

"Now that we've got that settled, you two ought to get on out there and answer to that crowd," Annie insisted. "There're TV cameras and radio stations and all sorts of dimwits asking stupid questions."

"You ready for this?" Sullivan squeezed her hand.

Mindful of their audience, Jo went up on tiptoe and placed a gentle kiss on his lips. "With you by my side, I can take on the world."

* * * * *

Look for the second book in Marin Thomas's
Hearts of Appalachia *miniseries*
IN A SOLDIER'S ARMS
Available in February 2008
Only from Harlequin American Romance

HARLEQUIN® *Romance*®

New York Times bestselling author

DIANA PALMER

Handsome, eligible ranch owner Stuart York knew
Ivy Conley was too young for him, so he closed his heart
to her and sent her away—despite the fireworks between
them. Now, years later, Ivy is determined not to be
treated like a little girl anymore…but for some reason,
Stuart is always fighting her battles for her. And safe in
Stuart's arms makes Ivy feel like a woman…his woman.

Winter Roses

Available November.

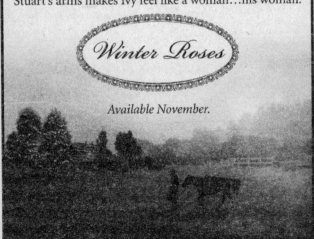

Mediterranean NIGHTS™

*Not everything is above board
on Alexandra's Dream!*

*Enjoy plenty of secrets, drama and sensuality
in the latest from Mediterranean Nights.*

Coming in November 2007...

BELOW DECK

by

Dorien Kelly

Determined to protect her young son,
widow Mei Lin Wang keeps him hidden
aboard *Alexandra's Dream* under cover of
her job. But life gets extremely complicated
when the ship's security officer, Gideon Dayan,
is piqued by the mystery surrounding this
beautiful, haunted woman....

REQUEST YOUR FREE BOOKS!
2 FREE NOVELS PLUS 2
FREE GIFTS!

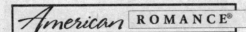

Heart, Home & Happiness!

YES! Please send me 2 FREE Harlequin American Romance® novels and my 2 FREE gifts. After receiving them, if I don't wish to receive any more books, I can return the shipping statement marked "cancel." If I don't cancel, I will receive 4 brand-new novels every month and be billed just $4.24 per book in the U.S., or $4.99 per book in Canada, plus 25¢ shipping and handling per book and applicable taxes, if any*. That's a savings of close to 15% off the cover price! I understand that accepting the 2 free books and gifts places me under no obligation to buy anything. I can always return a shipment and cancel at any time. Even if I never buy another book from Harlequin, the two free books and gifts are mine to keep forever.   154 HDN EEZK 354 HDN EEZV

Name _____ (PLEASE PRINT) _____

Address _____ Apt. # _____

City _____ State/Prov. _____ Zip/Postal Code _____

Signature (if under 18, a parent or guardian must sign)

Mail to the **Harlequin Reader Service®:**
IN U.S.A.: P.O. Box 1867, Buffalo, NY 14240-1867
IN CANADA: P.O. Box 609, Fort Erie, Ontario L2A 5X3

Not valid to current Harlequin American Romance subscribers.

Want to try two free books from another line?
Call 1-800-873-8635 or visit www.morefreebooks.com.

* Terms and prices subject to change without notice. NY residents add applicable sales tax. Canadian residents will be charged applicable provincial taxes and GST. This offer is limited to one order per household. All orders subject to approval. Credit or debit balances in a customer's account(s) may be offset by any other outstanding balance owed by or to the customer. Please allow 4 to 6 weeks for delivery.

Your Privacy: Harlequin is committed to protecting your privacy. Our Privacy Policy is available online at www.eHarlequin.com or upon request from the Reader Service. From time to time we make our lists of customers available to reputable firms who may have a product or service of interest to you. If you would prefer we not share your name and address, please check here. ☐

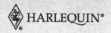

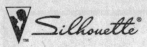

Romantic
SUSPENSE

**Sparked by Danger,
Fueled by Passion.**

Onyxx agent Sully Paxton's only chance of
survival lies in the hands of his enemy's daughter
Melita Krizova. He doesn't know he's a pawn in the
beautiful island girl's own plan for escape. Can
they survive their ruses and their fiery attraction?

*Look for the next installment in the
Spy Games miniseries,*

Sleeping with Danger

by Wendy Rosnau

Available November 2007 wherever you buy books.

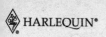

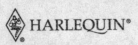
COMING NEXT MONTH

**#1185 THE PERFECT TREE by Roz Denny Fox, Ann DeFee
and Tanya Michaels**

There's something magical about sitting in front of a roaring fire, breathing
in the rich sights and smells of a beautifully decorated Christmas tree. This
holiday season, join three of your favorite Harlequin American Romance
authors in three stories about finding love at a special time of year—and
about finding the perfect Christmas tree.

#1186 DOWN HOME CAROLINA CHRISTMAS by Pamela Browning

Carrie Smith has seen her share of clunkers drive into her gas station in Yewville,
South Carolina, but never has anything like movie star Luke Mason in his Ferrari
shown up at the pump. And no matter how hard the sexy movie star tries to
persuade her otherwise, she's positive Hollywood and Hicksville will never meet!

#1187 CHRISTMAS AT BLUE MOON RANCH by Lynnette Kent

Major Daniel Trent came to south Texas to be a rancher, although
Willa Mercado doubts the injured veteran can handle the physical challenges
of the life. She bets he'll back out of buying part of her ranch before their
three-month agreement is up. But Daniel has every intention of spending
Christmas—and the rest of his life—with Willa and her kids at Blue Moon.

#1188 ALL I WANT FOR CHRISTMAS by Ann Roth

Tina Morrell has her hands full when a dear family friend needs her help just
as Tina's career in the cutthroat world of advertising takes off. But there's a
surprise waiting for her back home on Halo Island—a single dad and a little
girl who want to show her what the holiday season is really about....

www.eHarlequin.com

HARCNM1007